CHAPTER 1

"What a mess!" said the first clone trooper, CT-8863, as he surveyed the wreckage of the Separatist battleship *Malevolence* through his helmet's polarized T-visor.

"That's putting it mildly," said the second clone trooper, CT-4012. He turned his own helmeted head to let his gaze sweep over the area. "It's a very, very big mess!"

The third clone trooper, CT-5177, looked around but said nothing. This didn't surprise the others because CT-5177 seldom spoke at all.

The three troopers were virtually identical. Each wore a black, pressure-sealed body glove that was covered by white plastoid armor, with matching utility belts that carried handheld comlinks, grappling hooks, explosive grenades, and spare blaster magazines. They all moved and held their DC-15 blaster rifles the same way. Even their voices, transmitted via their helmets' built-in comm units, sounded alike.

In fact, their similarities extended right down to their genetic structure. They had been grown in cloning tanks and trained on the planet Kamino in order to serve and defend the Galactic Republic.

They were standing on a nameless, airless moon near the Kaliida Nebula, with their *Nu*-class attack shuttle resting on the scorched ground just a short distance away.

A day earlier, the moon had been a barren wasteland, but that was before Jedi General Anakin Skywalker had sent the *Malevolence* crashing into it. Now, massive metal fragments and countless bits of twisted, smoldering debris lay scattered in all directions across the lunar terrain.

"Too bad General Grievous got away," said CT-8863. Leveling the barrel of his blaster rifle at a shredded section of the *Malevolence*'s hull, he added,

"At least this battleship and its ion cannon can be crossed off our list of worries."

"You know the old saying," said CT-4012. "*The bigger they are . . .*"

" *. . . The bigger they explode!*" CT-8863 finished with a chuckle. CT-4012 joined in the laughter while CT-5177 merely nodded his helmeted head.

As the laughter ended, CT-4012 noticed a cylindrical scrap of metal near the toe of his right boot. He brought his foot down hard and crushed the scrap, driving it into the ground. Behind his helmet, he said, "I'll bet Grievous is crying droid tears right now over his broken toy."

Unexpectedly, a voice said from behind, "Don't forget that this 'broken toy' destroyed dozens of Republic warships and killed thousands of allies."

The three clone troopers turned to see who had spoken. It was their commanding clone officer, Captain Lock, who was walking toward them from the attack shuttle. They snapped to attention.

Lock's armor was scuffed and scratched, and his battered helmet was decorated with jagged blue markings. Lock was a veteran of the Battle of Geonosis, the first skirmish between the Republic and Separatist armies, which had launched the interstellar conflict that was already known as the Clone Wars.

Lock came to a stop before the three troopers. "If you're waiting for me to say, 'At ease, men,' you can wait until this war is over. Our orders are to recover debris samples to confirm a report that the enemy battleship was built by Quarren Separatists at the Pammant Docks. I'm told Chancellor Palpatine himself is eager for this confirmation. Is that understood, shinies?"

"Sir! Yes, sir!" answered the troopers, including CT-5177. They all knew that Chancellor Palpatine was the elected leader of the Galactic Republic. They also knew what *shinies* meant: clone troopers like them, who still wore shiny armor because they had yet to be in combat.

"And another thing," Lock added. "Calling you by your designation numbers takes too long. If you can't come up with proper names for yourselves, I'll be the one giving out nicknames. Understood?"

"Sir! Yes, sir!"

"Then let's get cracking," Lock said. "The sooner we find what we're looking for, the sooner we can leave this rock."

The troopers and Lock fanned out and began sifting through the rubble. They moved carefully and cautiously, always staying within sight of each other as they searched for debris with any kind of markings.

After nearly an hour of this tedious work, CT-4012 picked up a mostly pulverized piece of metal. He turned it over in his hands, examined it closely, then held it high over his head as he said, "Score!"

Lock and the other troopers trotted over to see what CT-4012 had found.

He held out the piece of scrap so all could see the engraved insignia on its surface.

"Well, I'll be," Lock said. "The insignia for the Free Dac Volunteers Engineering Corps! If that doesn't confirm the battleship was built at Pammant, I don't know what does. We'd better deliver this to Coruscant immediately."

He clapped CT-4012's shoulder plate and said, "You've got sharp eyes, soldier. Maybe your nickname should be Sharp."

"Sharp?" CT-4012 repeated, testing the sound of it.

"Nothing wrong with 'Sharp'," Lock said. "It's a good name."

"Thank you, sir," said the trooper formerly known as CT-4012, his voice filled with pride.

"Let's move out," Lock said, motioning to the others to return to the shuttle.

As they walked, CT-8863 noticed a partially melted circuit board in a nearby pile of debris that he'd missed earlier. The board's exposed assembly was as exotic as it was intricate, distinguished by overlapping patterns of concentric silver rings. CT-8863 stopped to bend down and pick it up. "Sir!"

Lock, Sharp, and CT-5177 stopped in their tracks. Looking at the object in CT-8863's hand, Lock said, "What is it? More evidence of Pammant construction?"

"No, sir," said CT-8863. "That is, I don't think so, sir."

"Then why are you showing it to me?"

Hearing the impatience in Lock's voice, CT-8863 answered quickly. "Sir, I don't recognize this board as anything used by either the Separatists or the Republic."

Behind his helmet, Lock lifted his eyebrows skeptically. "You can recognize circuit boards at a glance?"

"Yes, sir," CT-8863 said. "Studying circuitry is, uh, sort of my hobby. I've never seen an assembly like this. It might mean the Separatists have a new ally that we don't know about."

Lock looked at the circuit board again. "The Jedi will probably want to have a look at it," he said. He lifted his gaze to CT-8863. "You have sharp eyes, too, but I won't have a pair of Sharps under my command. Because of your interest in technology, we'll call you Breaker."

"Breaker, sir?" CT-8863 said doubtfully. "Sorry, I don't understand. Are you suggesting that I enjoy breaking technology?"

Lock rolled his eyes. "Breaker is short for circuit breaker."

"Oh."

"It's a good name!"

"Yes, sir!" said the newly named Breaker, who hadn't meant to question his superior officer. "Thank you, sir."

Turning to face CT-5177, Lock said, "As for

you, I've got a fine nickname picked out for—"

Lock was interrupted by a rapid burst of blaster fire. A volley of energy bolts traveled from the nearest debris pile and slammed into CT-5177, sending him falling backward.

Before CT-5177 hit the ground, a battle droid lifted its damaged frame away from the debris. Sparks flew from the droid's left hip joint as it lurched forward, angling its blaster rifle at the other troopers.

"Die, clone scum!" the droid said as it squeezed off another burst.

Lock, Sharp, and Breaker did not pause to wonder how the droid had survived the battleship's crash. Such thoughts were not part of their training and conditioning. They responded automatically and without fear, moving quickly to swing their rifles into position and return fire on the droid.

The droid fired one burst that glanced off the armor at Sharp's right shoulder. Sharp grunted at the impact but kept firing his own weapon. The droid's body jerked and spun as a hail of energy bolts sheared off its head and arms. The droid's body collapsed and its head bounced across the ground.

The bouncing head cried out, "Aw, nuts!"

Captain Lock and Breaker scrambled over to CT-5177's fallen body. Sharp kept his rifle trained on the droid's head until it rolled to a stop.

Facing Sharp sideways from the ground, the head repeated, "Die, clone scum!"

Sharp blasted the metal head to smithereens.

CT-5177 wasn't moving. At least one of the droid's shots had pierced the silent clone's armored chest plate. Captain Lock placed his black-gloved hand on the side of CT-5177's collar, then said, "He's alive! Let's get him back to the ship. Move!"

CT-5177 moaned as the others lifted and carried him up the attack shuttle's ramp and into the main cabin. As they entered, Captain Lock used his elbow to hit a button on the wall.

There was a loud *wham* as the hatch slammed shut behind them, followed by a rushing sound as compressed air quickly flowed in to fill and pressurize the cabin. CT-5177 moaned again as the troopers placed him on the metal deck.

The shuttle's clone pilot already had the engines running when Lock said, "To the *Demolisher*! Now!"

The *Demolisher* was the Republic Star Destroyer that had delivered the attack shuttle to the moon's orbit. As the clone pilot deftly worked the controls, the shuttle lifted from the ground and its wings dropped into flight position. Then the shuttle turned its nose skyward and rose rapidly into space, heading for the waiting Destroyer.

The troopers worked fast on CT-5177. Sharp maneuvered a laser tool to shear through the wounded trooper's plastoid armor and body glove to expose his chest. Breaker removed CT-5177's helmet and slapped a transparent respirator over his mouth. Lock pulled off his own helmet as he grabbed an emergency medpac and snapped it open.

CT-5177 blinked as his helmet came off. He tried to focus on Lock's face. Like all clones, he had inherited the rugged, swarthy features of his genetic template, a bounty hunter named Jango Fett. CT-5177's forehead was covered by a sheen of sweat.

Looking at the wound on CT-5177's chest, Breaker said, "What a mess."

"That's an understatement," Sharp said. He glanced at Lock and said, "Will he live, sir?"

"No one dies unless I order them to die!" Lock said as he slapped a wide medpac over CT-5177's chest. Then he stared hard into his eyes and said, "Tell me, soldier. You're not ready to say your last words, are you?"

Under the respirator, CT-5177 gasped, "No, sir."

"Good! Because if you don't stay alive, you'll never know your nickname!"

CHAPTER 2

Chancellor Palpatine leaned forward in his chair so he could have a closer look at the thing that had been placed on his desk in his suite at the Senate Office Building on the planet Coruscant. The thing was an exotic but obviously damaged circuit board, the same one that Captain Lock's squad had recovered from the *Malevolence*'s crash site a day earlier.

Raising his gaze to the tall, silver-haired man who had delivered the circuit board, Palpatine said, "Are you certain of this device's origin?"

"Yes, Chancellor," said the Jedi Master Ring-Sol Ambase. "The clone squad that found it was unable to identify its manufacturer, so they sent it to Jedi

Archives. I happened to be in Archives when it came in."

"And your records confirmed that it came from KynachTech Industries on Kynachi?"

"There was no need to consult records. I am very familiar with the design of technology manufactured by KynachTech. It is a personal interest. I was born on Kynachi."

Palpatine sighed. "Please, do forgive me, Master Ambase. I was under the impression that the people of Kynachi have golden hair, and I had not considered your ancestry."

"An apology is unnecessary, Chancellor," Ambase said. "The Kynachi are indeed distinguished by their hair, a characteristic that is partially the result of the Kynachi diet. Naturally, because I have spent most of my life on Coruscant, I do not share this trait."

"Yes, naturally," Palpatine said. "In any event, I can assume you are aware that KynachTech Industries has always insisted on manufacturing technology for entirely peaceful purposes?"

Ambase nodded.

"Then how did a KynachTech circuit board

wind up on a Separatist battleship?"

"As of now, we can only speculate."

Palpatine frowned. "It's been nearly ten years since the Kynachi chose to become isolationists and severed ties with the Republic. Since then, they have refused to allow trade or respond to any of our transmissions." His brow furrowed, and then he said, "I don't suppose you have had any recent contact with your family on Kynachi?"

"I am a Jedi," Ambase said. "I have had no contact with my biological family since I was an infant."

Palpatine shook his head sadly. "Of course. Forgive me, I should have known better than to ask. Still, you know a good deal about your homeworld?"

"It is a Jedi's duty to be familiar with many things. Granted, there's not much to know about Kynachi. To the best of my knowledge, KynachTech Industries is the *only* industry on the planet except for farming."

Palpatine rose from his desk and moved to the wide window that offered a sweeping view of Galactic City, the most expansive megatropolis in the galaxy.

As afternoon air traffic glided past his window, Palpatine said, "I was not surprised to learn that the battleship with the ion cannon was built at Pammant, but to discover that Kynachi was somehow involved . . . This is most distressing." He sighed. "Kynachi may be very remote, and her people may have chosen isolation, but I remember it as a lovely, peaceful world. I fear that Kynachi has joined or become occupied by the Separatists."

"There are other possibilities," Ambase said. "Perhaps the Kynachi are unaware that KynachTech supplied technology to the Separatists. Perhaps the technology was stolen."

"I had not considered that." Palpatine looked away from the window to face Ambase. "But how are we to discover the truth without violating their isolation agreement or endangering the Kynachi people? How can we learn whether they need or want our help?"

Ambase was silent for a moment, then said, "A Republic ship might not be welcomed at Kynachi. An investigation would have to be very discreet. A small, covert task force, a Jedi with twelve troops, could travel by unarmed freighter to investigate KynachTech."

"Unarmed?" Palpatine said with surprise. "Is that wise?"

"If the Separatists are already at Kynachi, and we show up in a Republic gunship, we might draw their attention immediately."

Palpatine sighed. "Yes, I suppose an unarmed freighter does have a tactical advantage," he said. "Would you be willing to lead this mission?"

"Chancellor, that's not my decision to—"

"But, Master Ambase, I'm sure the Jedi Council will concur that you, with your knowledge of Kynachi, would be the best choice. I will contact Master Yoda and Master Windu at once." Before Ambase could protest, Palpatine continued, "If no one objects, might I also encourage you to consider the troops for your command?"

"You have a team in mind?"

"Yes," Palpatine said. "The squad who recovered the debris from the Separatist battleship and delivered it to you. They strike me as *most* resourceful."

After leaving the Senate Office Building, Ring-Sol Ambase took a diplomatic shuttle to the Jedi Temple, an enormous structure topped by five tall spires. He went directly to the Temple's holographic training area, which was engineered for Jedi and Padawans to practice their lightsaber skills.

He made his way past several Padawans who were testing their non-lethal training lightsabers against various simulated opponents until he found a young male Jedi, a humanoid alien boy with blue skin and red eyes, who stood before holograms of three super battle droids.

The boy had hung his dark brown, hooded robe on a metal peg that jutted out from a nearby wall. He was clad in a tan tunic with matching leggings, and wore a synthetic leather utility belt and boots.

The holograms of the hulking, slope-shouldered droids raised their arms to open fire with their dual laser cannons, launching crimson energy bolts at the boy. He made a series of swift, sweeping chops through the air as his training lightsaber connected with the bolts, batting them back at the holograms.

The young Jedi had no difficulty sending a dozen bolts straight back at his attackers before he spun and leaped at them. Still in midair, he swung his blade to chop off the gun arms of two droids, then swung again as he landed on the floor, severing the droids' legs with his lightsaber. As the two droids collapsed, the third droid swiveled fast to take aim and fire at its moving target.

An energy bolt whizzed past the boy's head, but he ducked and rolled toward the last standing droid. He twisted his wrist to flick his lightsaber up through the droid's midsection, cutting it in half. As the droid's torso fell, though, his right gun arm fired.

"Stang!" the boy cursed as one of the fired energy bolts traveled straight into his right thigh. Because the energy bolts, like the droids, were merely three-dimensional constructions of light, they did not cause any physical harm, but the boy was discouraged just the same. The disabled droid fired again, trying to hit the boy but instead launching a spray of bolts at the ceiling. Rising from the floor, the boy said, "End program."

As the holographic droids vanished and the youth deactivated his training lightsaber, Ambase said, "You're improving, Nuru."

Nuru Kungurama turned his gaze to the silver-haired Jedi. He bowed and said, "Thank you, Master."

"However, please refrain from swearing. Such language is not becoming of a Jedi."

"Sorry, Master," Nuru said with another bow. Clipping his training lightsaber to his belt, he walked over to Ambase and said, "May I ask how your meeting went with the Chancellor?"

"I have been given an assignment," Ambase said. Anticipating Nuru's next question, Ambase added, "During my absence, you shall continue your training here at the Temple."

Nuru lowered his gaze to the floor.

"Do not be disappointed, Padawan. My mission may be dangerous. As capable as you are, you are still too young for combat. You understand that, don't you?"

"Yes, Master," Nuru said. Raising his eyes to meet Ambase's, he added, "But I still wish I could go with you."

Ambase studied the boy's expression, then said, "You're concerned . . . that I might not return?"

Nuru nodded. "Just as Master Skaa did not

return from Geonosis."

Ambase sighed as he thought of the terrible battle that had begun the Clone Wars.

"I miss your former Master, too," Ambase said. "We lost many friends on Geonosis. But if we are to honor their sacrifice, we must do what we can to help preserve and protect the Republic. Which is why I must go."

"Thank you for coming to tell me," Nuru said. "When Master Skaa left for Geonosis, he did so without saying good-bye to me. I realize that it may have made no difference if he had, but—"

"If there had been more time," Ambase interrupted, "Master Skaa would have said farewell. You know that."

Nuru was silent for a moment, then said, "When do you leave?"

"Immediately. A clone squad is waiting for me now."

"I look forward to your return, Master."

"As do I, my Padawan," Ambase said. He clapped the boy on the shoulder, then turned and walked off, moving past the other young Jedi trainees as he headed for the holographic training area's exit.

As Ambase walked away, Nuru looked at the other trainees. He knew that five of them had recently lost their first Masters, too. Watching Ambase's departing form, he wondered if he would ever see the Jedi again. And then, unexpectedly, he felt a sense of impending doom.

Nuru knew that the Force—the universal energy that gave the Jedi their power—could sometimes speak to a Jedi.

He was certain that this was such a moment. He no longer wondered whether he would ever see Master Ambase again. He was certain that Ambase would never return to Coruscant.

Unless he had some help.

Nuru grabbed his hooded robe and ran to the nearest Jedi trainee, Nat Lariats, a female Nautolan with fourteen long tentacles extending from the back of her head.

"Here, Nat," Nuru said as he handed his training lightsaber to her. "You can have this."

Confused, Nat said, "Why are you giving it to me?"

"Because I already built a real one," Nuru said.

Reaching into one of his robe pockets, he withdrew another lightsaber, which he promptly clipped to his belt. Before Nat could ask any more questions, Nuru pulled on his robe and ran after Ambase. But as he ran, Nuru kept his distance.

He didn't want Ambase to know he was following him.

CHAPTER 3

"Look alive, Breaker and Sharp!" Captain Lock called from across the hangar in the Jedi Temple. "And say hello to your old pal!"

Breaker and Sharp were standing beside an old freighter that rested in a wide hangar within the Jedi Temple. They were already suited in their armor, except for their helmets, which they held at their sides. Both troopers turned to see Captain Lock approaching from across the hangar, with CT-5177 at his side, walking without any apparent discomfort.

Breaker smiled. "Good to see you on your feet again, CT-5177."

CT-5177 responded with a nod.

Gesturing to CT-5177, Lock said, "I think the medics set a new record, the way they patched him up good as new." Then he gave an expectant look at CT-5177 and said, "Go on, tell them the nickname I gave you."

CT-5177 winced slightly, then muttered, "Chatterbox."

"Ha!" Sharp laughed. "That's a good one!"

"I don't get it," Breaker said. "CT-5177 hardly ever talks."

Lock smirked. "It's called *irony*, Breaker. Chatterbox is an *ironic* nickname."

Before Breaker could ask Lock to explain the meaning of irony, Ring-Sol Ambase entered the hangar. Seeing the silver-haired general who would lead their mission, Lock and the three clone troopers snapped to attention. Ambase came to a stop in front of them and said, "Captain Lock?"

"Greetings, General Ambase," Lock said. "The freighter you requested is ready for departure."

"And the rest of the task force?"

"Already on board, sir. A complement of two additional four-man squads and two pilots."

"Very good," Ambase said. "I would like to

express my appreciation to the trooper who found the circuit board. Is he among them?"

"Breaker's right here, General," Lock said as he aimed a thumb at Breaker.

Ambase bowed his head to Breaker and said, "You are to be commended for realizing the board was an unusual design. I was informed that you study technology as a hobby?"

"Yes, General."

"Most interesting," Ambase said before turning for the freighter's boarding ramp. "I'll brief the entire team on our way to our destination."

Breaker was the last of the troopers to follow the Jedi into the freighter. He was about to raise the boarding ramp and seal the hatch when he saw a blue-skinned boy dressed in Jedi robes, running fast across the hangar, coming straight for the ramp. As the boy came up the ramp, he waved his fingers at Breaker and said, "You never saw me."

"I never saw you," Breaker said, his mind clouding under the young Jedi's power. The boy slipped past Breaker and quickly concealed himself in a nearby utility closet.

Without any memory of the boy, Breaker raised

the ramp, shut the hatch, and then proceeded through a low-ceilinged corridor to the main cabin, where the other troopers and General Ambase were already strapped into their seats. As Breaker strapped himself in across from Ambase, Ambase looked at him and said, "That's strange . . . I just had the feeling that my apprentice is nearby."

Breaker smiled and said, "I can assure you that you're the only Jedi on board, General."

A moment later, the freighter lifted off, and flew out of the hangar. It rose away from the Jedi Temple, climbing over the spires of Coruscant's highest skyscrapers until it left the atmosphere and proceeded into space.

The Duros bounty hunter was seated at a table in his shabby hotel room on Coruscant. His broad-brimmed hat tilted back on his head while he cleaned his blaster pistols, as the compact holoprojector activated.

The bounty hunter lifted his red-eyed gaze to the air above the holoprojector as the device suddenly produced a flickering blue-light image of a cowled figure.

It was the Sith Lord Darth Sidious.

"Cad Bane," Darth Sidious said, biting the words off with his grating rasp. "I require your services."

"I'm all ears," Bane said, which was something of a joke, because his bald, blue-green head was smooth at the sides. His hands continued their work on the pistols while his eyes remained fixed on the hologram.

"A freighter has just left the Jedi Temple," Darth Sidious said. "It is bound for Kynachi, and carries a Jedi General with a clone trooper task force."

"What do you want of me?"

"That depends on who survives."

"Jedi, huh?" Bane said. "My fee just went up. A lot."

"You will be well compensated," Darth Sidious said. "Go to Kynachi immediately. I will contact you with further instructions."

The hologram flickered off. Less than a minute later, Bane left the room, taking his guns with him.

CHAPTER 4

"Is something wrong, General Ambase?" Breaker said.

Although Breaker was not an expert on the emotional behavior of any life form, he had noticed the way that Ring-Sol Ambase had been staring out the freighter's viewport, watching the brilliant cascade of lights as the freighter traveled through hyperspace. His brow was furrowed, which Breaker believed was an indication that the Jedi was concerned or irritated.

Right after the freighter had made the jump into hyperspace, Ambase had briefed the clone task force about their mission: They were to serve as his emergency backup while he investigated the KynachTech facility on Kynachi.

During the briefing session, Ambase had not exhibited any obvious concern about the mission. Now, as he looked away from the viewport to face Breaker, he said, "It's my apprentice."

Confused, Breaker said, "You're . . . worried about him?"

"Even though we're already many parsecs away from Coruscant, I still have the strangest feeling that he is close by."

Suddenly, there came a thudding sound accompanied by laughter from the main cabin, where Sharp and three other clone troopers were engaged in a contest to see who could do the most push-ups while wearing all their armor. The thudding sound came from the chin areas of the competing troopers' helmets, which struck the deck as they lowered themselves, and the laughter came from those watching them.

Ignoring the noise from the main cabin, Breaker faced Ambase and said, "The freighter was thoroughly inspected before we left the Jedi Temple, General. No one boarded except us."

Ambase nodded. "You assured me of that earlier. Still, I have this nagging feeling of his presence. I wish I could explain it."

Hoping to help, Breaker said, "We can't send any transmissions while traveling through hyperspace, but when we reach Kynachi, would you like to contact the Jedi Temple and confirm that your apprentice is all right?"

"If a transmission can be sent without jeopardizing the mission, I would appreciate it."

"We'll make it a priority," Breaker said. He was about to return to the main cabin, but then he caught himself and said, "General, if you don't mind my asking, why didn't your apprentice join you on this mission?"

Fixing Breaker with a quizzical expression, Ambase said, "You are a curious fellow, Breaker. But no, I don't mind you asking. My Padawan, Nuru Kungurama, is still quite young and has never seen combat. I only recently became his Master, after his first Master died at the Battle of Geonosis. Unfortunately, my duties as a General have prevented me from spending much time with Nuru."

Reflecting on this, Ambase said, "I wonder . . .

this feeling I've been having since we left the Temple. Perhaps it is the Force itself at work here, trying to tell me that I should have brought Nuru with me."

"The Force, General?" Breaker said. "I really wouldn't know anything about that."

"Jedi are not the only ones who draw their power from the Force, Breaker," Ambase said. "The Force flows through all living things. Even you and your fellow clones."

"I'm glad you think so, General."

Just then, a red light flashed on and off at the edge of the viewport.

Seeing the light, Breaker said, "Time to strap in again. We're about to drop out of hyperspace."

They returned to the main cabin, where Captain Lock studied a navigation console while the other troopers settled into their seats and secured their helmets.

Sharp said, "Hey, Breaker! You should have seen it. Chatterbox came in second place. Knuckles did more push-ups than any of us."

"Told you he'd win," said another clone. "Knuckles does push-ups in his sleep."

"Yeah?" Sharp said. "I bet Chatterbox would

beat him at a quiet contest. Chatterbox doesn't even snore!" This comment brought on another round of laughter.

"All right, cut the chatter," Captain Lock said. Turning to Ambase, he said, "I'm going up front with the pilots. Be right back."

While Lock headed for the freighter's bridge, Ambase lowered himself into his seat. Belting himself in, he surveyed the identical troopers.

Although it remained something of a mystery how the Kamino cloners had been commissioned to create an army to serve the Republic, Ambase could not help but admire the clones' courage and camaraderie.

"Which of you are Knuckles and Chatterbox?" Ambase asked.

"I'm Knuckles, sir," one of the troopers said amiably as he secured a set of polarized macrobinoculars to his helmet. Chatterbox raised a black-gloved hand and casually saluted Ambase.

"I'm sorry I didn't see your contest," Ambase said with a smile. "When this mission is done, perhaps you'll have a rematch."

The troopers responded with enthusiastic nods.

There was a shuddering sensation as the freighter exited hyperspace and the sublight engines kicked in. The freighter was still shuddering as it emerged in realspace, in orbit of the planet Kynachi. But before the shuddering could stop, the entire ship was rocked by violent explosions.

None of the troopers showed a trace of fear as their bodies jolted against their seats. Reacting quickly and automatically, they placed their helmets over their heads, checked their seat belts, and braced themselves.

"We're under attack!" Captain Lock's voice sounded over the freighter's comm. "Kynachi's surrounded by what looks like a Trade Federation blockade! Droid fighters incoming at—!"

Lock's words were cut off by a second explosion, which was followed by a rippling series of smaller blasts.

There was a roar of wind. Alarms blared. Lights flashed. Every man on the freighter knew the ship's hull had been breached. Breaker grabbed an emergency breath mask and handed it quickly to Ambase, who drew it up over his face.

Sharp consulted a sensor in his helmet. "General

Ambase, we've lost communication with Captain Lock and the pilots."

All the seated troopers turned their helmeted heads to the Jedi General.

"To the escape pods," Ambase said. "Now!"

CHAPTER 5

Ambase and the clone troopers scrambled out of their seats. Another series of explosions rocked the freighter, knocking some of the troopers off their feet. An inner wall blew open, launching wide chunks of metal that crushed and killed two troopers instantly.

The power of the blast sent Knuckles tumbling down the corridor that led to the main hatch, where he saw a utility closet door fly open and a young, blue-skinned boy fall out.

Knuckles didn't recognize the boy or know how he got on board, but he immediately assumed he was a Jedi by his robed attire and the lightsaber on his belt. "Hang on!" Knuckles said as he grabbed for the boy, whose cheeks were puffed out as he held his breath in the rapidly thinning air. The boy clutched at Knuckles's armored forearm and held tight. Knuckles braced his weight against the corridor wall, then flung himself back into the main cabin, taking the boy with him toward the escape pods.

Laser fire hammered at the ship, cutting through the hull and killing another trooper. Ambase, Sharp, and four more troopers raced into one escape pod and the pod's hatch slid and a blast shield shut behind them.

Breaker was about to follow Chatterbox into a second pod when he saw Knuckles approaching with a boy clinging to his arm. Although Breaker had no recollection of his earlier encounter with the boy, he instantly recalled his conversation with Ambase, and suspected that the boy was Ambase's Jedi apprentice.

Breaker gestured to the pod's open hatch. "In here!"

While Knuckles moved forward with the boy and air whipped at their bodies, Breaker suddenly realized that Ambase's pod had failed to jettison. He looked to a viewscreen beside the sealed blast shield. On the viewscreen, he saw Ambase, Sharp, and four other troopers within the pod.

"Controls are jammed," Sharp said via his helmet's comm unit. "Can you release us?"

Another bombardment of enemy laser fire struck the freighter. Breaker kept his balance as he threw open the cover to the emergency control box above the hatch to Ambase's pod. Breaker saw a neatly severed cable, and realized in an instant that someone had cut power to the pod's automatic release latches.

Nuru was still holding his breath as he clung to Knuckles. As they approached Breaker, Nuru sighted the nearby viewscreen, which displayed his Master seated in the disabled pod. Knowing better than to open his mouth, Nuru called out with his mind: *Master!*

On the viewscreen, Ambase's expression went wide with surprise. He turned his gaze so that he appeared to be staring straight through the blast shield that separated him from his apprentice. *Padawan?!*

Breaker was oblivious to the silent exchange

between the Jedi. He pushed aside the severed cable in the control box. Without any idea of whether the manual release would even work, he wrapped his fingers around a lever and pulled down on it hard.

There was a muffled explosion as the disabled pod's separator charges detonated. The pod rocketed away from the freighter, whisking Ambase and his fellow passengers toward Kynachi.

Knuckles hauled Nuru into the open escape pod, where Chatterbox quickly slapped a breath mask over his face. Breaker was about to follow Knuckles into the pod when he saw another trooper stumble toward him from the shambles of the main cabin.

The trooper was clutching at his midsection. His armor was severely scorched, but jagged blue markings were still visible on his helmet.

"Captain Lock!" Breaker said. "We thought we'd lost you."

Lock gasped. "Better luck . . . next time, Breaker."

"Someone tampered with the auto-release systems, sir," Breaker said as he broke open the control box above the remaining pod. "You get in. I'll stay behind to release the pod manually."

Still clutching at his side, Lock lurched closer. He came to a stop when he arrived beside Breaker, peered into the pod, and saw the boy wearing a breath mask, sitting beside Chatterbox and Knuckles.

"Where," Lock stammered, "did this Jedi . . . come from?"

Knuckles said, "I found him."

Lock wheezed. "Lucky you."

"Sir," Breaker said. "Get in before we—"

Lock shoved Breaker into the pod, then stepped back as he hit a button to seal the hatch and blast shield. He didn't know whether his helmet's comm unit was still working, or if Breaker and the others could hear him, but as he reached up to access the controls for the pod's manual release, he said, "Until I'm dead . . . I'm the one . . . who gives the orders."

Lock almost slipped as he pulled the lever, but he clung to it with the last of his strength. There was a loud clacking sound, and then the second escape pod rocketed away. Lock slumped against the blast shield, angling his helmet to peer at a nearby viewscreen. He saw the pod tearing off toward Kynachi.

A moment later, there was one final explosion, and the freighter and everything on it was gone.

Breaker, Chatterbox, and Knuckles didn't have time to ask the boy to identify himself or explain his presence on the freighter. They were too busy clinging to the belts that held them in place against the pod's circular seat as they fell fast past the armada of dagger-winged droid starfighters.

Knuckles angled his head to glance through the viewport, which offered a spiraling view of the exploding freighter. The droid starfighters had only retreated slightly to avoid the wide spray of debris from the obliterated ship, but they were already swinging around to pursue the pod.

Knuckles said, "Where's Ambase's pod?"

Breaker hastily checked a console that should have allowed them to track the other pod. "Don't know. The console's not working," Breaker said. "Neither is the transponder for the distress signal." He reached up to whack the side of his helmet. "My helmet's long-range comm isn't working. Yours?"

Knuckles and Chatterbox checked their own built-in comms. "Ours are down, too," Knuckles said. They checked the handheld comms at their belts and found them similarly inoperative.

"We're cut off," Breaker said. "Totally."

Before anyone could comment further, the pod was slammed hard sideways. All four occupants knew that enemy fire had skimmed the pod's energy shield. Sparks showered out from the useless console near Breaker, then blossomed into flames. Chatterbox pulled an extinguisher off the wall, popped the trigger, and sprayed the fire until it was out.

Breaker tore the thin plastoid protective cover off another console. "Autopilot's been disabled." He tugged off his gloves, then began pulling at wires, trying to sort out their connecting points to a circuit board.

There was a bright flash of brilliant light outside the viewport as the pod struck and penetrated Kynachi's atmosphere. The pod streaked downward through thick, gray clouds without slowing, diving straight for the planet's surface.

Watching Breaker dig into the exposed console, Knuckles asked, "What are you doing?"

"Trying to extend our lives," Breaker said, his fingers working fast at the wires.

Knuckles glanced again through the viewport to catch a dizzying glimpse of what looked like a wide expanse of rocky terrain. "Try faster."

A spark ignited near Breaker's fingers in the console. "Got it."

A loud blast sounded from outside, the welcome noise of the pod's maneuvering jets kicking in. The pod began to rotate as it fell, trying to right itself before landing, but the engine made a loud whine that sounded anything but stable. Knuckles threw a protective arm over Nuru and said, "Brace yourself."

The pod dipped through the air, hit the ground at a slight angle with an ugly, bone-jarring thud, then bounced and rolled. The main thrusters died at the same time as the maneuvering jets broke off.

As the pod tumbled across the planet's surface, Knuckles said, "What a ride!"

The pod skidded and spun until it finally came to a stop. It lay on its side, and its passengers heard a steady pattering sound against the hull. They looked through the hatch's viewport, which faced up toward the sky, and saw heavy sheets of rain coming down.

Knuckles looked at the boy. "You all right?"

The boy nodded.

"We need to get out," Knuckles said as they removed their seatbelts and secured their weapons. "Hurry. Those fighters will be here any second."

Breaker punched a control stud to open the hatch, but the hatch remained closed. "It's jammed." He was about to strike the control stud again when he felt something press down on top of his armored shoulder. It was the long, black barrel of Chatterbox's blaster rifle, which Chatterbox was aiming at the hatch.

Knuckles said to the boy, "Cover your ears."

Breaker turned his face away from the hatch but kept his body still. Chatterbox squeezed the rifle's trigger.

There was a loud blast and the hatch exploded outward. The three troopers and the boy spilled out of the pod along with the blaster fumes, taking their weapons with them.

They found themselves standing on the hard surface of a small, shallow basin, surrounded by short hills that resembled permanently frozen waves. Rainwater spattered and streamed all around them. "Careful," Breaker said. "It's slippery."

The troopers kept their helmets on, but the boy removed his breath mask and flung it back into the pod. Knuckles snapped his macrobinoculars down over his visor to scan the rain-swept area. "126 meters in that direction," he said, pointing. "Small plastoid structure with trees for cover. No life forms."

The sound of a sonic boom came from overhead, signaling the approach of the enemy fighters. Breaker said, "Run."

They bolted from the wrecked pod. Rain pelted the troopers' armor while the boy's robes became quickly drenched. Despite his own warning, Breaker nearly slipped on the slick ground.

Knuckles glanced at the boy to make sure he didn't fall behind, but then the young Jedi had a sudden burst of speed, running so fast that it appeared his boots barely touched the ground.

Knuckles leaped over a wide puddle in his effort to keep up. A few more steps and the ground changed from hard, slippery rock to mud. Beyond the noise of rainfall and their clomping boots, they heard the distinctive scream of the incoming fighters, growing louder with each passing second.

The boy was the first to reach the structure, a

long hut without windows, situated amid a grove of dark green trees. Drawing the lightsaber from his belt, he activated its brilliant blue blade and drove it through the hut's thin plastoid wall, then flicked his wrist to make a wide, circular cut.

He switched off the lightsaber and was about to place a kick to the cut area when Knuckles arrived at his side and kicked first, knocking the circular sheet of plastoid into the building.

Following the boy's lead, the three troopers scurried through the hole in the wall. Inside, they found two narrow aisles of shelves lined with large sacks and variously sized storage containers. A series of small vents in the ceiling were the structure's only source of illumination, but it was enough to enable them to see a sliding door on the opposite wall.

The smell was awful. Scrunching his nose, Nuru realized it was coming from the sacks. They were fertilizer bags.

Knuckles peered through the hole. "I see five starfighters," he said. "Wait. One is landing."

He watched as a droid starfighter reconfigured its wings, unfolding and extending them into long, sharp-tipped legs while it slowed its thrusters. It had barely touched down when its legs began skittering, causing it to slip and collapse against the uneven, rain-soaked ground with a loud crash.

Hearing the noise outside, the boy said, "What happened?"

Knuckles said, "Wait."

The droid hauled itself up, pivoted on one leg, then fired its thrusters as it transformed back into its flight configuration and sailed up into the stormy sky. The other starfighters shot up after it.

"They're retreating," Knuckles reported as he moved away from the wall. "The ground's too slick for them to land, at least for now."

"They'll be back soon enough," Breaker said. "And if they determine we escaped the pod, this building will be the first place they'll search. We can't stay here."

Just then, a mechanical voice spoke: "Intruder alert!" The group turned to see a small, spherical security droid emerge from one of the aisles to hover in the air before them. The droid was an old model with a bent antenna, and its compact repulsorlift hissed as it drifted closer. Focusing its grimy photoreceptors on the trespassers, the droid said,

"You are not authorized to be in—"

"Stand down, droid," Breaker said. "We have authorization. Show him, Chatterbox."

Chatterbox spun his blaster rifle in his hands, seizing it by the barrel and swung it as hard as he could at the hovering droid. The rifle's butt smashed into the droid, shattering it in midair. Its pieces fell to the floor.

The boy was startled by the clone's violent action. "Why'd you do that?" the boy said. "The droid might have helped us!"

"We couldn't take that chance," Knuckles said. "Officially, we're not on this planet. That droid might have compromised our mission."

"This mission is already compromised," Breaker said. "Think about it. Our freighter's life pods were sabotaged. And the moment we dropped out of hyperspace, those starfighters were ready for us."

Unexpectedly, it was Chatterbox who spoke next. "Someone set us up."

Then Chatterbox slowly turned his helmeted head to face the boy, who was shrugging out of his wet robe.

"I wish I hadn't left that breath mask behind,"

the boy said. "It really stinks in here."

Knuckles and Breaker turned their own heads to follow Chatterbox's gaze. All three troopers were holding their blaster rifles so that the barrels were aimed toward the warehouse ceiling, but they shifted their weight slightly within their armor, bracing themselves for the unexpected as they studied the boy.

Although the clones were trained to serve and obey their Jedi commanders, they also knew that their greatest enemy, the Separatist leader Count Dooku, was a former Jedi. They did not rule out the possibility that Dooku had secret allies in the Jedi Order.

The boy was trying to wring the water from his robe's sleeves when he realized the troopers were looking at him.

"What's wrong?" he asked.

When they didn't immediately answer, he took a cautious step backward, and accidentally stepped on a fragment of the old security droid that the least talkative clone had destroyed.

Staring hard at the boy through his visor, Knuckles felt his muscles tense.

"By the way you handled that lightsaber of yours," he said, his voice remarkably calm, "we don't doubt that you're a Jedi. But may we ask what exactly you were doing on the freighter?"

CHAPTER 6

The young Jedi did not fear the three troopers. He was even confident that he could evade or disable all three of them if necessary. But he was surprised by how quickly their manners had changed.

When the freighter was under attack, they had rescued him without question. Now, even though their helmets concealed their faces, he could feel their eyes boring in on him with intense suspicion. He said, "You think I'm somehow responsible for what happened?"

"I didn't say that," Knuckles said, his body still as a statue. "I asked . . . What were you doing on the freighter?"

The boy kept very still, keeping his eyes fixed on Knuckles's visor. While rain drummed down on the plastoid roof above their heads, he said, "I snuck onboard the freighter just before you left Coruscant. My Master wanted me to stay at the Temple, but . . . I had a feeling that something might go wrong. I was hoping to help him."

Knuckles said, "Can you prove that claim?" He asked the question politely, but it still sounded like a challenge.

Before the boy could answer, Breaker noticed something a short distance behind the boy. Thinking fast, he said, "General Ambase told me his apprentice was Heckle Wiriest. Is that you?"

"Heckle who?" Nuru said, confused. He shook his head. "Sorry, no. I mean . . . I can't imagine why Master Ambase told you that. I'm his apprentice. My name is Nuru Kungurama."

"You just passed the test," Breaker said as he relaxed his grip on his blaster rifle. Turning to the other troopers, he said, "I'll vouch for him. The General told me Kungurama's name earlier. Claimed he sensed his apprentice's presence on the ship."

But Knuckles was also confused. "Test?" he said.

"Who's Heckle Wiriest?"

Breaker said, "I just spotted the words on that bag over there." He pointed to a yellow bag marked *Heckle Wiriest Fertilizer* on a shelf behind Nuru.

Knuckles and Chatterbox immediately relaxed, too. Knuckles said, "That was a clever way to make sure the boy was telling the truth, Breaker."

"Well," the boy said, "you could have just *asked* me my name. I would have told you . . . Breaker?"

Breaker nodded. "That's me." He gestured to the other troopers. "He's Knuckles. He's Chatterbox."

Knuckles said, "Sorry to question you like that, Commander Nuru. We just had to be sure you were on the level."

"Of course," Nuru said somewhat warily. "Now, I don't know what your mission was, but . . . Breaker, you're the one who rewired the pod to save us, right?"

"Affirmative."

"Is there any way you can contact my Master's pod or send a message to the Jedi Temple?"

Breaker shook his head. "Our helmets have long-range comms, but they're not working. Even if they were, they wouldn't be able to transmit all the way back to the Temple. As for our mission, we were assigned to help General Ambase find out whether a company called KynachTech deliberately supplied parts for a Separatist battleship."

"But now that my Master is missing," Nuru said, "you'll help me find him. Right?"

Breaker glanced at Knuckles and Chatterbox, then returned his gaze to Nuru. "Under ordinary circumstances, Commander, that would be our first priority. But this mission was compromised. We don't even know whether the other pod made it to this planet. We need to find a way to contact the Jedi Temple and summon reinforcements."

"My Master, he is still alive," Nuru said. "I know it."

"How? Do your senses detect him?"

Nuru was silent for a moment, then said, "No, I can't sense him. But Master Ambase must have survived. I know he would have found a way."

"We'll discuss this later," Knuckles said firmly. "If we're anywhere near this building when those starfighters return, we're as good as dead. But we can't be seen walking out in the open with our armor on." He looked to Breaker and Chatterbox. "We need to wear camouflage."

Chatterbox stepped over to the nearest shelf, picked up a bag of fertilizer, and emptied its contents onto the floor. What he did next made Nuru gasp.

It was still raining outside as the four hooded figures moved away from the storage shed on Kynachi. The smallest figure tried to keep his distance from the others.

"Good thinking, Chatterbox," Knuckles said as they trudged along the edge of a farm that lay beyond the shed. "These cut-up bags make fine cowls and robes. We look just like refugees or journeymen laborers."

"You look more like three fertilizer sacks wearing clone trooper boots," Nuru said. Indeed, the troopers remained fully armored under the fetid bags, and openly carried their blaster rifles. "If you're lucky, someone might mistake you for bulky bounty hunters."

"Nothing wrong with bulky," Knuckles said.

Nuru squinched his nose. "You really stink."

"That's not a bad thing, either. People will stay away from us."

"People?" Nuru said, rolling his eyes. "Microbes will stay away from you!"

"Even better," Knuckles said.

They arrived at the edge of a wooded area and then proceeded into it. Nuru glanced at Breaker and said, "The troopers who were in my Master's escape pod. Did you know them all well?"

"Chatterbox and I only served with one of them before, the one we call Sharp."

Knuckles said, "I served with the others. Trueblood, Close-Shave, Dyre, and No-Nines. All good men. Why do you ask?"

"I was just wondering," Nuru said. "I do think it's interesting how you all distinguish each other. I mean, you're identical. How do you tell who's who?"

"Very carefully," Knuckles said, grinning behind his helmet.

Nuru couldn't tell if Knuckles was joking. Before he could comment, he heard a noise from overhead. "The droid starfighters!" he said. "They're coming back!"

Nuru and the clones ducked and took cover behind a cluster of trees. They peered back the way they came, past the trees that grew at the farm's outer edge.

Although their position prevented any view of their abandoned escape pod, they could still see the storage shed that had served as their temporary refuge. A moment later, the starfighters came into view, descending from the clouds.

The starfighters leveled off, then circled over the area beyond the shed, where the escape pod had crashed. Looking away from the starfighters, Breaker turned to face Nuru and said, "It won't take them long to figure out we're gone. We should keep mov—"

"Look!" Nuru said.

Breaker followed Nuru's gaze to see the distant starfighters launching laser fire at the planet's surface. Past the shed, a plume of fire and smoke rose and blossomed. Despite the distance, the explosion's flash was so bright that Nuru squinted his red eyes. Barely three seconds later, the sound of the explosion reached his ears as a series of crackling bursts.

The starfighters continued circling for another

minute, then tore off, leaving thin trails of smoke across the sky as they headed south. When they were no longer in sight, Knuckles glanced at Chatterbox and muttered, "I think it's safe to say they destroyed the pod."

Chatterbox nodded.

Rising from his hiding spot behind the tree, Breaker looked back at Nuru and said, "Ready to move on, sir?"

"Yes." Nuru lifted his gaze to the smoke trails of the departed starfighters. "I just hope my Master is all right."

"Don't worry," Knuckles said. "He's in good hands."

CHAPTER 7

"General Ambase?" Sharp said as he blinked his eyes open.

The clone trooper couldn't see anything, only darkness. Because of the pressure across his armored chest and the way his knees were bent, he believed he was still belted into his seat in the escape pod. From the steady but off-kilter gravity, he also sensed that the pod was no longer falling, that it had come to a rest somewhere.

His helmeted head felt heavy, and there was a bitter taste in his mouth. Moving his hands to his collar so he could check the pressure seals, he realized his arms felt heavy, too.

Sharp's gloved fingers gripped something unexpected, a sheet of flexible fabric that seemed to be draped over him.

Pulling it off his head, he saw through his visor that he was clutching an insulated blanket. One of the pod's storage compartments had broken open and spilled out blankets and other emergency supplies.

Turning his head slightly, he surveyed the pod's dim interior. None of the pod's control switches or lights were on, and the main console was an exploded mess.

A thin shaft of light poured in through the pod's viewport, which angled up toward a gray sky. Sharp could make out the forms of his five fellow passengers—four fellow troopers and their Jedi leader, all motionless in their seats.

Ring-Sol Ambase's head was slumped to the side, an emergency breath mask secured over the lower half of his face.

"General Ambase!" Sharp said as he removed his seat belt.

Once freed, he reached out to Ambase, gently placing his gloved fingertips against the man's neck. He found himself holding his own breath as he felt for a pulse.

Just then, the clone named Dyre shifted in his seat beside Ambase. Dyre tilted his head back to look up at Sharp. Sounding dazed, he said, "The general! Is he—?"

"He's alive," Sharp said, removing his fingertips from Ambase's neck.

"What happened?" Dyre said groggily as he unbuckled his seat belt.

"We landed."

"We all . . . passed out?"

Sharp nodded, and the slight motion made him dizzy. "Pod sensors . . . are off-line. I think . . . there's a gas leak." He quickly yanked the breath mask off of Ambase's face.

Dyre said, "What're you doing?!"

"Our air supply . . . it's fouled," Sharp said. "Might be toxic."

As Sharp reached for a control button near the hatch, Dyre said, "Wait! We don't know . . . can we breathe what's out there?"

"If we landed on Kynachi . . . we'll breathe," Sharp said. "If not, we're dead." He struck the button and popped the hatch, which opened with an explosive hiss. Cool, fresh air flooded into the pod, followed by a trickle of water. Sharp peered through the hatch and commented. "Rain."

"Must be Kynachi," Dyre said. "Any idea of what region?"

"None," Sharp said as he pulled off his helmet and took a deep breath of air.

Gesturing to the wrecked control console, Dyre said, "No point looking for answers there."

Just then, Trueblood, Close-Shave, and No-Nines began to stir in their seats. Sharp glanced at Dyre and said, "Check on them while I take a look outside."

Sharp placed his helmet back over his head, readied his blaster rifle, and then eased through the hatch. Rain pattered against his armor as he lowered himself down to the hard ground.

The battered pod had come to rest on a long, narrow stretch of ground that lay beneath two steep, rocky walls. A shallow stream of rainwater flowed over Sharp's feet and traveled down the length of the gorge, which was littered with large, ovoid stones.

Overhead, all he could see of the sky was a long and ominous strip of gray clouds, bordered by the tops of the facing cliffs.

From his education on Kamino, he was certain he was standing at the bottom of an ancient riverbed. He adjusted his helmet's sensors, scanned the area, and confirmed that the nearest cliff wall was fifteen meters high.

Looking upstream, he saw a series of staggered ledges along the wall to his left. The ledges looked climbable.

Clacketty-clack.

The sound came from four meters to Sharp's left. He spun fast, swinging his rifle to aim its barrel in the general direction of the noise. He found himself aiming at a small creature that stood beside a puddle on the rain-spattered ground. It was an arthropod with a segmented body.

Two antennae extended from its blunt head, and its naturally armored external skeleton had a dusty color that blended easily with the surrounding rocks. It stood on four spindly legs and raised an equal number of pincer-tipped arms. Without warning, it flexed its pincers.

Clacketty-clack.

The creature appeared to be relatively harmless,

but Sharp kept his rifle trained on it as he took a step forward. It reacted by skittering sideways, making a tapping sound against the ground as it moved downstream, away from Sharp.

When it reached a rock that rested about thirty meters from the pod, it ducked behind the rock and vanished.

Because the creature didn't appear to pose any threat, Sharp slung his rifle over his shoulder and then climbed back into the pod. He found Dyre had carefully removed the three other troopers' helmets. Trueblood, Close-Shave, and No-Nines looked up at Sharp as he entered, rainwater dripping off his armor.

Nodding toward the revived troopers, Dyre said, "They're all right. Just winded. No broken bones."

"We landed in a ravine," Sharp said as he removed his helmet. "Steep walls. Might make us slightly hard to find while it's raining, but we're exposed from above."

"See anything unusual?"

"A small life form. A four-clawed crustacean."

"Harmless?"

"It darted off. Seemed afraid of me."

Dyre grinned. "Better that than the other way around."

Close-Shave shook his head and muttered, "My skull . . . feels like it's filled with rocks."

"It'll pass," Sharp said. "Just keep taking deep breaths. I'm not sure what happened, but I'm guessing the attacking starfighters ruptured a gas hose in our pod's life-support system." He turned his gaze to Ambase's unconscious body.

Trueblood followed Sharp's gaze and said, "Why hasn't the general recovered?"

"Beats me," Sharp said, "but it could be because his physiology isn't the same as ours. We're different."

"Maybe not just different," Dyre said. He thumped his right fist against his chest plate and added, "Maybe we're tougher."

Sharp leveled his gaze at Dyre. "I doubt you'd be saying that if our superior officer were conscious."

"Sorry," Dyre said. "I meant no disrespect. Just hoping to boost morale."

"Well, save the pep talks for *after* we've blasted the clankers who brought us down."

No-Nines scowled. "That ambush couldn't have

been an accident. The droids were waiting for us in orbit. How'd they know when we'd arrive?"

Trueblood said, "Maybe we were set up. Maybe someone sabotaged our pod."

"I'm afraid we'll have to save speculations for later, too," Sharp said as he unlocked Ambase's seat buckle. "The droids must be searching for us. If we stay put, this pod will be our coffin."

He slid back a seat cushion to reveal a storage compartment. It contained a number of supplies, including an emergency medpac, a waterproof tent, and a collapsible stretcher.

The troopers pulled on their helmets. No-Nines, Trueblood, and Close-Shave exited with their weapons, leaving Sharp and Dyre with more room to maneuver within the pod. Sharp clipped the medpac to his belt alongside two grenades.

Dyre extended the stretcher into a locked position and rested its upper end out through the hatch. They wrapped Ambase in blankets, secured him to the stretcher, and covered him with part of the tent to keep him dry. The unconscious Jedi didn't make a sound or shift a muscle as he was carried out into the rain.

The stretcher-bearers, Sharp and Dyre, stepped away from the pod, walking carefully to avoid slipping on the ovoid stones.

While No-Nines kept his visor directed upstream and Close-Shave looked downstream, Trueblood lowered his gaze from the sky to face Sharp and Dyre as they came to a stop beside him. Trueblood said, "Which way?"

Sharp tilted his helmet to his right and all the troopers began walking upstream. When they reached the series of ledges that Sharp had seen earlier, Sharp came to a stop. The others did the same. Sharp looked at No-Nines and said, "Climb to the top, scope the area, and report back."

The troopers' rifles were equipped to fire not only energized plasma bolts but also ascension cables that terminated with grappling hooks. No-Nines raised his rifle and fired, launching his rifle's cable upward.

The grappling hook snared the ledge at the top of the cliff, and then No-Nines set his weapon to slowly reel in the cable. Gripping the rifle with both hands and keeping its barrel aimed at the sky, he planted one foot on the wall and then began scaling the cliff's face.

As No-Nines ascended and rain continued to fall, Dyre adjusted his hands on the stretcher's grips. Looking at Sharp, Dyre said, "For all we know, there's an army of droids waiting for us up there. Might be safer to stay in this ravine. If we find any overhangs or caves, we might take shelter until we— "

Clacketty-clack.

The noise came from behind, near the abandoned escape pod. Responding to the noise, Sharp and Dyre held tight to the stretcher as they turned their heads, while Close-Shave and Trueblood spun fast with their blaster rifles.

No-Nines heard the clacking noise, too, and paused to look down. All the troopers sighted a four-clawed creature that stood about three meters away from the pod. One of the creature's antennae twitched.

Keeping his voice low, No-Nines said from above, "Everyone all right?"

Dyre responded with an affirmative hand gesture, and No-Nines resumed climbing. Keeping his gaze on the creature, Dyre said, "Sharp, is that the thing you saw before?"

"I'm not sure," Sharp said. "It looks . . . bigger."

A rumbling sound came from the stream. Suddenly, dozens of ovoid stones shifted on their own, sending up sprays of water as they rolled over and extended pincer-tipped appendages to reveal they weren't stones at all.

Clacketty-clack, clacketty-clack-ck, CLACK, CLACK!

The clacking noise echoed loudly through the ravine. Trueblood said, "What in the blazes?"

Keeping his voice calm, Dyre said, "Steady, boys. They might just be defending their territory, and shooting at them might alert the enemy to our loca—"

A thunderous ripple suddenly drowned out Dyre's words, and the entire stream erupted violently. The troopers stood motionless as hundreds of ovoids moved like a wave, and then the ovoids transformed, rapidly unfurling into clawed crustaceans.

Some of the creatures were directly beneath the empty escape pod, and they thrashed and undulated with such force that the pod began to rock back and forth upon their thick-shelled backs. This action was followed by the ugly sound of metal being crushed and shredded.

"Look at them!" Close-Shave said. "They're tearing into the pod like it is a snack!"

The nearest creatures snapped their claws menacingly at the troopers. Trueblood said, "What was that talk about staying in the ravine and not shooting?"

Dyre chuckled. "That's history."

Several creatures skittered forward. Close-Shave and Trueblood shot at the ground in front of them, trying to drive the creatures back. Three of the monsters didn't stop and were blasted on the spot. There was surprisingly little blood. The others paused for just a moment, then lurched forward again.

Sharp craned his neck back to view the trooper on the cliff. "No-Nines! Move!"

No-Nines climbed faster, his cable retracting into his rifle with each step.

Trueblood and Close-Shave kept firing at the creatures while Sharp and Dyre faced the wall and braced the stretcher against their utility belts, allowing each of them to hang onto the stretcher with one hand while leaving the other hand free to draw their rifles. They raised their weapons and fired at the same time, sending their ascension cables past No-Nines to the uppermost ledge.

The instant Sharp and Dyre felt the grappling hooks take hold, they quickly repositioned their bodies, moving closer together and shifting the stretcher so Ambase rested across their midriffs. Then they each moved both hands to grip their respective rifles and began following No-Nines up the cliff, carrying Ambase with them.

No-Nines reached the top of the cliff, letting his grappling hook snap back into place below the end of his rifle's barrel. Turning fast, he angled his weapon down as he gazed past the ascending Sharp and Dyre to see Trueblood and Close-Shave backing toward the wall.

Trueblood and Close-Shave were blasting everything that moved in front of them. No-Nines wasn't sure how many shots they had already fired, but from his vantage, he knew they wouldn't last two seconds if they paused to reload with fresh energy packs. He took aim and began squeezing away at his own trigger.

Trueblood and Close-Shave saw the fresh hail of energy bolts that sailed down from above and slammed into the encroaching creatures. Taking advantage of No-Nines's sniping, they elevated their rifles to launch their ascension cables up past the sides of Sharp and Dyre, who were almost at the top of the cliff.

The instant Trueblood and Close-Shave's grappling hooks took hold, they started chasing the others up the wall. The creatures snapped viciously at their heels. Before the troopers could breathe a sigh of relief, the creatures surged toward the base of the cliff and began piling up on top of each other.

Trueblood felt a claw whack the back of his left leg and glanced down to see the creatures scrambling up and over one another to reach him and Close-Shave. While No-Nines continued firing from above, Trueblood swung one foot to kick at the rising heap of deadly creatures.

"Keep moving!" Close-Shave shouted.

Both Sharp and Dyre kept their gaze forward, ignoring the rain that pelted their visors as they maintained a synchronized pace up the cliff. They knew that just one wrong step could unbalance the stretcher they carried and send Ambase crashing to his death.

"No-Nines!" Dyre said through clenched teeth. "Give us a hand!"

No-Nines shifted his rifle to one hand and continued firing as he came down on one knee on the ledge above Dyre and Sharp. He extended his free hand to grab the edge of the stretcher and pulled, yanking the stretcher off of his allies and onto the ledge. A moment later, Dyre and Sharp heaved themselves up beside No-Nines and collapsed beside the stretcher.

Still gripping his rifle in one hand, No-Nines continued firing down at the growing pile of crustaceans beneath Close-Shave and Trueblood when the pile suddenly swelled, carrying the creatures higher.

No-Nines tore a grenade from his belt, popped the clip, and let the grenade fall past Close-Shave and Trueblood. The ascending troopers saw No-Nines's actions and climbed even faster.

The grenade bounced off the backs of several creatures before it detonated. The explosion incinerated the nearest creatures and pulverized dozens more, and the shock wave launched Close-Shave and Trueblood skyward. They twisted their bodies in midair, angling to land on the ledge beside No-Nines, and crash-landed hard but unharmed.

A plume of smoke rose up from the bottom of the cliff. The surviving creatures made a horrible screeching sound as they fled, skittering back into the shadows of the ravine.

The smoke was still rising as No-Nines turned away from the ledge. He saw Sharp and Dyre kneeling beside the stretcher, checking on the still-unconscious Jedi, as Trueblood and Close-Shave pushed themselves up to their feet. He also saw something else.

"Incoming."

A squad of Separatist vulture droid starfighters descended from the rain clouds, heading toward the troopers.

"The explosion must've attracted them!" Close-Shave said.

"We can't retreat into the ravine," Trueblood said. "There's too many of those things still down there."

Dyre chuckled. "I never liked retreating,

anyway." He checked his blaster rifle's ammo pack and added, "Bring on the droids."

"We have to protect the general," Sharp said as the starfighters drew closer. He pointed to a rocky outcropping twenty meters away. "Come on."

Sharp, Dyre, Trueblood, and No-Nines each used one hand to grip the stretcher while holding their rifles in their other hands. They lifted Ambase and ran for the outcropping. Close-Shave ran after them but kept his eyes on the incoming starfighters.

The troopers were still running for the rocks when the vulture droids opened fire.

CHAPTER 8

Nuru, Breaker, Knuckles, and Chatterbox walked through the woods until they arrived at the top of a hill that offered a wide view of the rain-shrouded region. Knuckles pushed back the cowl of his makeshift robe and lowered his macrobinoculars over his visor to scan through the rain. "That way," he said, pointing. "A settlement. No air traffic."

Breaker faced Nuru and said, "General Ambase informed us that Kynachi stopped allowing visitors to their world ten years ago. The spaceport is the most populated area, but no matter where we go here, we're likely to attract attention simply because we're strangers."

Nuru said, "What should we do?"

"You're the Jedi," Knuckles said. "You tell us."

Nuru was surprised by Knuckles's words. He suddenly realized that the troopers were looking at him not as a boy, but as their new commander. He thought for a moment. "Well, I think it would be best if we don't all walk into the settlement together at the same time. I'll go in with one of you."

Breaker said, "Which one?"

"You just volunteered," Nuru said. "You can keep your blaster pistol under that thing you call a robe, but you'll be less conspicuous without your rifle and helmet."

Knuckles said, "What should Chatterbox and I do?"

"Watch our backs," Nuru said. "Stay close to me and Breaker, but not too close."

"Will do," Knuckles said. Chatterbox nodded once in agreement.

Breaker handed his rifle to Knuckles, then pulled back his cowl and removed his helmet. As rain spattered on his bare head, he said, "Commander Nuru, I don't mean to sound rude, but . . . I believe *you'll* be the one who might attract the most attention. I know little about Kynachi, but from what General Ambase told me about the indigenous people, I suspect red-eyed, blue-skinned beings such as you are quite unusual."

"I'm a Chiss," Nuru said matter-of-factly. "Chiss are unusual throughout most of the galaxy. But I'll do my best to stay unnoticed." He adjusted his cowl to conceal most of his face.

Breaker said, "What if someone asks how we arrived on Kynachi?"

"Trust me, Breaker," Nuru said. "The way you smell right now, no one will get close enough to ask."

"We don't get strangers here much," said one of the two young men who suddenly blocked the doorway of the trading post that Nuru and Breaker had been about to enter.

"Yeah," said the man's accomplice. "Especially strangers that smell like poodoo."

Rain had turned to drizzle by the time Nuru and Breaker arrived at the settlement, a cluster of shabby, old buildings with small windows. Most of the buildings were made of baked mud, but some had cheap plastoid additions. Despite the weather, there were a few dozen Kynachi natives outside the settlement's trading post, where vendors were selling food and other goods from tarpaulin-covered carts.

Nuru and Breaker had hoped to gather information at the trading post before the two men stopped them. The men wore ratty clothes and had foul breath. Nuru also noticed that both men had remarkably golden hair. One man had a gold mustache. The other had a scar across the bridge of his nose.

Breaker had clipped his helmet to the armor plate behind his left shoulder, and it bulged under his robe at his upper back. "I'm a farmer," Breaker said, hoping that this explanation would be sufficient to explain the stench of his robe. "I mean, I *was* a farmer. I'm looking for work."

"Well, mister, you look to me like you're a hunchback," said the man with the mustache. "And you just brought your hunchbacked self to the wrong place. Didn't you see the sign on your way into town? It says, NO POODOO-STINKIN' FARMERS ALLOWED."

The scarred man snickered at the same time as the mustached man reached for something in his pocket. Breaker was about to make a move that would break one man's arm and the other's nose when Nuru said, "We don't want trouble."

"We don't want trouble," the mustached man echoed with a slack expression as he removed his hand from his pocket.

"No trouble," the scarred man said. "No trouble at all." Neither had any idea that the boy was manipulating their minds.

Nuru said, "We have to go now."

"We have to go," the men said in unison as they sauntered off.

Breaker said, "That was close."

Nuru looked up to Breaker and said, "You really do stink. Maybe you should wait outside while I go in and ask—"

"Hey!" a woman's voice called out. "You two!"

Nuru and Breaker turned to see a woman walking toward them from the food vendors. She wore a synthetic leather poncho, and had a set of goggles wrapped tightly around the crown of her black rain hat.

Like the departing men, she also had golden hair, which she had cut short. In her left hand, she clutched a large bag that contained vegetables she'd just bought from a vendor. As she approached, she said, "I noticed Wevil and Namnats hassling you, and was just coming over to see if you needed help. What'd you say to make them back off like that?" She came to a stop in front of Breaker, but then she caught the smell of his robe and took a step back.

Breaker said, "I beg your pardon, ma'am?"

"Stang!" the woman said, trying not to gag. "No wonder those jerks left you alone. Did you roll in something?"

Breaker shrugged. "I'm a farmer."

She gave him a skeptical look. "If you say so," she said. "But if I didn't know better, I'd say you two were a long, long way from home."

Nuru said, "What makes you think that?"

"I've gotten to know most people around these parts, but I don't recall anyone ever mentioning a boy with blue skin and red eyes. And I'd wager that if you two pulled your hoods back, I'd see neither one of you has gold hair."

"Oh," Nuru said. "Is gold hair common on Kynachi?"

The woman snorted. "Boy, you just said a mouthful. If you don't know that the food on Kynachi makes most people's hair turn gold, you must have just arrived, and without a tour guide."

Nuru turned to Breaker and said, "Did you know about the gold hair?"

Breaker nodded. "I was informed of that detail."

Nuru scowled. "Why didn't you tell me?"

"You didn't ask."

The woman cocked her head as her eyes flicked between Breaker and Nuru. "You're an odd pair," she said, and then she locked her gaze on the boy. "The way you talk to your tall friend here, I get the impression you're the one in charge."

Breaker said, "Don't be ridiculous. He's just a boy."

"That he is," the woman said. "And a most unusual looking one at that." Turning her gaze to Breaker, she said, "Tell me, what's your business on Kynachi?"

"I already told you," Breaker said. "I'm a

farmer."

"Yeah? Most farmers prefer less unusual footwear."

Nuru glanced at the mud-spattered white armor that covered Breaker's lower legs and feet. Breaker said, "I guess I'm just unusual."

"But not entirely," the woman said. "You're dressed just like your two shadows."

"Shadows?" Breaker said. "I don't know what you're talking—"

"I've been stuck on Kynachi for almost three years now," the woman interrupted, "and I've kept my eyes open. Also my nose. I couldn't see the faces of the two men who followed you into town, but their robes smell just as bad as yours. I lost sight of one of them, but the other is lurking in the alley to the left of the trading post." Then she looked to Nuru and said, "Your farmer friend isn't a very good liar. How about you?"

Nuru considered his options, then said, "We are indeed a long way from home. We're looking for friends of ours, but our comms don't work."

"Of course, they don't work," the woman said, "on account of the frequency-jammer tower at the spaceport. I guess you didn't know about that either?"

Nuru shook his head. "We really could use some help. Maybe there's some way we could help you, too?"

"I'm willing to listen," she said. "But as for helping you . . . Well, that depends on whether you can get me off this planet." Then she turned and said, "Get your two friends. My landspeeder is around the corner. We'll go to my place."

Breaker raised his hand and slowly rolled his fingertips to his palm, signaling to the other troopers to come forward. Chatterbox and Knuckles cautiously emerged from their hiding spots and headed after the others.

As the woman led Nuru and the disguised troopers to her landspeeder, one of the food vendors reached into his pocket and removed a small comm unit. Holding the comm close to his mouth, he said in a low whisper, "Can you hear me?"

The voice on the other end said, "I'm all ears."

Examining the comm, the vendor said, "Hey, you were right! This special comm of yours, it works in spite of the frequency jammer!"

"Just like I said it would," the voice said impatiently.

"You wanted to know if I saw any strangers in town?"

"Tell me who you saw."

"Three robed men and a boy," the vendor said. "Two of the men, I couldn't see their faces, but they're carrying blaster rifles. They're leaving with a woman who runs a diner at the spaceport, not far from your hotel."

"Give me directions to the diner," said Cad Bane.

"May I ask your name?" Nuru said from the rear seat as the landspeeder accelerated away from the settlement and zoomed over an open plain.

"What?" the woman said from behind her speeder's controls. She had lowered the speeder's canopy to diminish the noxious odor of her passengers, and the repulsorlift's engine made it difficult to hear.

"Your name!"

"Lalo Gunn!"

Breaker sat in the front passenger seat beside Gunn, holding her bag of vegetables on his lap, while Nuru was scrunched in back between Knuckles and Chatterbox, who still wore their helmets. Nuru said, "I'm Nuru Kungurama. This is Breaker."

"And your masked buddies?" Gunn said over her shoulder.

"The one on my left is Chatterbox, and the other is Knuckles."

The trooper to Nuru's left responded. "Actually, I'm Knuckles."

"Sorry," Nuru said.

As Gunn guided the landspeeder around a wide hill, she said, "Those are the dopiest names I ever heard."

Deciding to change the subject, Nuru said, "You've been on Kynachi almost three years? Why did you come to a world where visitors aren't welcome?"

"I was in the import and export business," she said. "I thought there was money to be made here. Boy, was I wrong. The Trade Federation controls everything here, including who comes and goes."

"We only just learned that ourselves," Breaker said. "We were under the impression that Kynachi chose to cut themselves off from the Republic."

"That's what I thought, too," Gunn said. "It's what the Trade Federation wants everyone to believe. They conquered this world ten years ago, and because Kynachi is so remote, no one in the Republic even noticed."

"Ten years ago," Nuru mused. "That would have been around the time of the Battle of Naboo. But why didn't anyone here call for help?"

"Remember the frequency-jammer tower I mentioned? The Federation set it up at the KynachTech factory to prevent transmissions to or from Kynachi."

Nuru said, "So, the Federation took over the factory?"

"That's right," Gunn said. "They use it to make droids and weapons."

"And circuit boards," Breaker muttered, recalling the device that had launched the troopers' secret mission.

"What?" Gunn said, then quickly added, "Never mind. It's too noisy with the canopy down. We'll talk more when we get to my place."

Twenty minutes later, Gunn's landspeeder approached the outskirts of Kynachi's only spaceport. Nuru could see the open-domed rooftops of the larger docking bays, which appeared to be surrounded by a wide sprawl of older buildings, similar to the ones he'd seen at the settlement. Except for a few ragged pedestrians, there was practically no one on the street.

Nuru said, "Where are all the people?"

"Most stay indoors," Gunn said. "It's the best way to avoid the droid patrols."

Gunn guided the speeder past a row of deserted, empty buildings. She brought the vehicle to a stop beside a shabby-looking, snub-nosed Corellian transport that rested on its landing legs.

On the ground beneath the elevated transport's lower hull were some spindly tables and chairs. A humanoid navigation droid with a single large central sensor node for a head was cleaning cheap drinking cups beside a hovering dining cart.

"Welcome to Gunn's Diner," Gunn said as she climbed out of her speeder, taking her bag of vegetables with her. "My ship used to be named the *Hasty Harpy*, but that was before we were grounded."

Noticing the transport's oversized thrusters and barely concealed laser cannon, Nuru said, "It looks like a smuggler's ship." He quickly added, "No offense."

"None taken," Gunn said. "Like I said: import and export."

"Oh."

Breaker said, "Is your ship operational?"

Gunn grinned. "She's ready for liftoff any time, but she wouldn't get far so long as that blockade's in orbit." She walked over to the droid beside the dining cart and handed the bag of vegetables to him. "The blinroots are for today's special, Teejay."

The droid took the bag and looked at the troopers and Nuru. Speaking in a bright, happy voice, the droid said, "How delightful! Shall I prepare a table for four?"

"Just rustle up some grub, nothing fancy," Gunn said. "We'll be in the main cabin."

The droid surveyed the empty seats and tables, and said sadly, "No one ever wants to eat outside."

Then he looked up and down the street,

confirmed that there wasn't anyone else in sight, and added, "It's a wonder that we're still in business at all."

Gunn rolled her eyes. "You're getting too emotional, Teejay. Keep it up, and I'll wipe your memory."

Breaker looked at Gunn and said, "That's a Genetech 2JTJ personal navigation droid, isn't it?"

"Used to be," Gunn said. "Now Teejay's a very frustrated waiter."

She lowered the transport's landing ramp and led Nuru and the three hooded men up through the hatch into the transport's main cabin, a spacious, low-ceilinged chamber with a cushioned bench and three seats.

"Dump your robes here," Gunn said at the top of the ramp. "I don't want you stinking up the whole place."

Breaker glanced at Nuru. Nuru said, "Go ahead."

The three troopers shrugged out of their robes and let them fall to the deck, revealing their white armor and weapons. Knuckles and Chatterbox still had their helmets on. Gunn looked the troopers up and down, then said, "Are you soldiers or something?"

Nuru said, "Don't you know about the Republic's clone troopers?" Nuru said. "Or the Republic's war against the Separatists?"

"War?!" Gunn shook her head. "I don't know what you're talking about. Thanks to the Trade Federation's frequency jammer, we don't get HoloNet News on Kynachi. I don't know anything about Separatists, but if you're fighting the Trade Federation, then I'm with you." She looked at the troopers. "Clones, huh? Do you all look alike?"

Nuru gave a nod to Knuckles and Chatterbox, prompting them to remove their helmets.

"Whoa," Gunn said as she looked at their faces. She glanced at Breaker, just to confirm that the three men were identical, then looked back to Nuru. "Now, that's something I've never seen before. How do you tell them apart?"

"Well, Knuckles has slightly broader shoulders."

Knuckles aimed a thumb at his chest and said, "I can do the most push-ups."

"That's nice," Gunn said without enthusiasm.

"And Chatterbox," Nuru continued, "well, he hardly ever says anything."

"Even nicer," Gunn said as she appraised the silent trooper. "I like men who keep their mouths shut."

Breaker and Knuckles were baffled by Gunn's comment. They looked at Chatterbox to see if he could offer an explanation, but he just shrugged.

Gunn faced Nuru and said, "So, if they're Republic soldiers, what exactly are you to them?"

Nuru blushed. "Well, I'm a Jedi. That is, I'm a Jedi apprentice, and my Master was—"

Nuru was interrupted by the distinctive sound of a rapid exchange of blaster fire. The noise came from outside the grounded transport. Startled, Nuru spun fast to look at the three troopers.

Knuckles said, "Doesn't sound good. Stay here, Commander!" Then Knuckles ran for the open hatch that led to the landing platform. He was only halfway down when he turned and came running back into the cabin. "Enemy droids!" he shouted as he readied his blaster rifle. "They spotted me!"

A moment later, there came a much louder blast from outside, and then a hunk of metal sailed up through the transport's open hatch and bounced off the main cabin's wall. The flying debris landed on the deck and rolled to a stop in front of Gunn's feet.

Everyone recognized the debris. It was the head of Gunn's navigation droid.

And then footsteps clanged against the landing platform. Nuru looked to the hatch and saw two pairs of lean, gunmetal gray droids coming in fast.

The four droids resembled Separatist battle droids but had truncated heads with white, glowing photoreceptors. The first pair carried black E-5 blaster rifles, and the second pair wielded shock-sticks.

Without hesitation, Nuru drew his lightsaber and ignited it.

CHAPTER 9

What happened next happened very quickly.

Knuckles and Chatterbox stepped in front of Lalo Gunn to shield her from the droids that had just entered the grounded transport's cabin. Gunn gasped as Nuru's lightsaber swept through the air at the same moment that the two blaster-wielding droids took aim at him and opened fire.

Nuru angled his blade fast, batting the speeding energy bolts back at all the droids. The droids staggered at the impact as their own blaster fire struck their torsos, but none of the droids lost their footing.

Nuru dodged another fired bolt after rapidly

calculating that its trajectory would slam into the cabin wall without striking Gunn or the troopers, and leaped forward to swing his lightsaber through the neck of the nearest droid.

Nuru's lightsaber swept through his first target and then chopped off the gun-arm of the second. He flicked his wrist and his lightsaber cleaved up through another droid's body and head, cutting it in half. The first two droids were still collapsing to the deck as the other pair raised the sharp, energized tips of their shock-sticks.

Nuru was about to attack the remaining droids when he suddenly felt a strong grip around his wrist. Breaker had grabbed him, and Nuru reflexively switched off his lightsaber as Breaker said, "Down!"

Breaker threw himself to the deck, pulling Nuru with him as he used his own armored body to shield the boy. They'd landed between the shock-stick wielding droids and the two other troopers.

Knuckles and Chatterbox instinctively selected their own targets and opened fire, sending energy bolts across the cabin, over the prone forms of their allies and straight at the two droids.

They fired at the droids' weapon-arms before shifting their aim to shoot at the droids' necks. The droids' bodies jerked and sparked and shattered before they fell to the deck like marionettes whose strings had been cut.

A silence fell over the transport's interior. Still covering Nuru, Breaker said, "Check outside."

Knuckles and Chatterbox leaped over the remains of the ruined droids, taking their rifles with them as they ran down the landing platform. They left Gunn crouched low against the wall in the cabin. She had her hands clamped over her ears as if she were expecting more noise.

Breaker rolled off of Nuru, pushing himself up from the deck. He offered his hand to the boy. Nuru ignored the hand and rose to his feet without help. He said, "Why'd you shove me?"

"I was protecting you," Breaker said.

Nuru secured his lightsaber to his belt. "I could've handled all the droids."

"Maybe," Breaker said, "but I couldn't take that chance."

Gunn removed her hands from her ears and stood up. Facing Nuru, she said, "When you told me you were a Jedi, I thought you were joking."

Nuru shrugged.

"I'm just looking for a way off Kynachi," Gunn continued. "I didn't bargain for dealing with a Jedi or getting my ship shot up by droid commandos." She glanced at Teejay's head amid the clutter of droid parts scattered on the deck. "Didn't bargain for losing my navigator, either."

Nuru said, "Droid commandos?"

"That's what these things are," Gunn said, placing a kick at a piece of gunmetal gray scrap.

Footsteps sounded on the landing ramp, and then Knuckles and Chatterbox reentered the cabin. They weren't alone. They had their arms wrapped around a humanoid male alien, whom they carried between them.

The alien had a long, green-blue face without a nose. At first glance, Nuru thought the alien was a Neimoidian, but quickly realized he was a similar-looking alien, a Duros, who was distinguished by larger eyes and a more prominent brow. The Duros wore a broad-brimmed hat, carried two holstered blaster pistols, and had his eyes squeezed shut.

Knuckles said, "No other droids outside, but we

found this guy lying on the ground."

The Duros lowered his head and said, "Take it easy! I'm blinded."

Breaker looked to Gunn and said, "Have you ever seen him before?"

"Never," she said. Lowering her voice, she added, "Judging from those quick-draw holsters he has strapped to his thighs, I'd say he's some kind of hired gun."

Knuckles and Chatterbox eased the Duros onto the cabin's padded bench, then turned to Nuru. Knuckles said, "Chatterbox and I will stand guard outside and watch for more droids."

Nuru nodded and the two troopers headed for the exit. They grabbed their smelly robes, pulled them over their armor, and stepped out of the transport.

Nuru moved beside Breaker and Gunn, who stood facing the Duros. The Duros tried opening his red eyes, then squeezed them shut again.

Breaker said, "Who are you, and what happened out there?"

"I'm a bounty hunter," Cad Bane said. "I stopped at the diner for a meal." He paused to catch his breath. "There was a droid outside . . . a waiter."

"This droid?" Breaker said, picking up Teejay's head and holding it in front of the Duros's face.

Bane opened his eyes slightly and squinted at Teejay's head. "It's blurry, but, yeah, I think that's him." He closed his eyes again and shook his head before he continued. "But then four droid commandos came from out of nowhere. I guess they were on patrol. They saw me and . . . they wanted to arrest me. I couldn't let them do that. I tried to run away, but they started shooting at me. I ducked behind a table for cover. The waiter, he ran off, and then . . . one of the commandos lobbed some kind of luma grenade. I didn't shut my eyes in time. Caught the full flash, but the blast missed me."

"Teejay wasn't so lucky," Gunn said. "You should be able to see again in a few minutes, bounty hunter. Meanwhile, tell us, what brought you to Kynachi?"

"A job," Bane said flatly.

"You'll have to do better than that, pal," Gunn said as she picked up one of the fallen droid commandos' blasters and pressed its barrel against the Duros's forehead. "No one has a job on Kynachi unless they're doing business with the Trade

Federation. For all we know, you're a Neimoidian spy."

Nuru said, "But he's not a Neimoidian. He's a Duros."

"Who said that?" Bane said, his eyelids fluttering. "Sounds like a kid."

"My name is Nuru."

"Well, you're right, Nuru. I am indeed a Duros."

Gunn pressed the blaster harder against the bounty hunter's forehead and said, "I don't care if you're King of the Hutts. I want to know how you got through the Federation blockade. And how come those droids wanted to arrest you."

Eyes still closed, Bane sighed. "I'm working for an enemy of the Federation. A very wealthy, powerful client I'd rather not name. My client provided pass codes to get my ship past the blockade, and also schematics for the prison at the KynachTech factory. I was hired to bust somebody out of the prison. I tried to keep a low profile, but the droids . . . I don't know. Maybe they didn't like the way I look."

Nuru looked at Gunn and said, "The KynachTech factory has a prison?"

"Courtesy of the Trade Federation, or so I've heard," Gunn said, pulling her blaster away from the Duros's forehead but keeping it aimed at him. "The factory is where they built the frequency jammer, too. The whole place is heavily guarded by battle droids."

Bane's eyes opened slightly, and then opened wider as he looked at Breaker. "I couldn't see you before, but . . . You're a Republic trooper!"

Breaker nodded. "That's right. So are the pair who hauled you in here."

Returning his gaze to Nuru, Bane said, "Then that means you must be . . . I'm sorry. I didn't realize I was talking to a Jedi. You could've used a mind trick to make me talk if you'd wanted."

Nuru shrugged. After Gunn had threatened the Duros with the blaster, he'd talked so readily that Nuru hadn't even considered trying a mind trick. Nuru said, "Who are you trying to get out of prison?"

"Out of respect to my client," Bane said, "I'd rather not say. But I assure you, the individual I'd hoped to liberate is no friend to the Federation or the Separatists." Bane paused, then said, "So, I guess you were hoping to break into the prison, too?"

Confused, Nuru said, "Why would you think that?"

Bane glanced nervously at the blaster in Gunn's hand. Nuru motioned for Gunn to lower the blaster. She did.

Bane sighed. "Well," he said, "about an hour ago, I was scoping out the prison, and I saw the droids escorting what appeared to be some new prisoners. Four Republic troopers. They were carrying a body. Looked like a man with silver hair, and he wasn't wearing white armor. I figured he might be a Jedi."

Now it was Nuru whose eyes went wide. He was almost afraid to ask, but the words tumbled out of his mouth. "Could you tell if he was still alive?"

Bane shook his head sadly. "Sorry," he said. "Not from where I was standing."

Breaker shook his head. "If you only saw four troopers, that means one of them didn't make it." He wondered if Sharp had survived.

Nuru looked at Breaker and said, "That may be. But Master Ambase is alive. I'm certain!" He looked back to the Duros. "You said you have schematics for the prison."

"Yes," Bane said. "The schematics are on a datatape."

"You know how to get in?"

"I do," Bane said. "And I thought I could do it on my own, but after seeing the place, I doubt it."

Breaker said, "What's the problem?"

Bane gestured to Gunn and said, "Like the lady said, the prison is guarded by droids. There's a main entrance and another for deliveries, both protected by energy shields. The delivery entrance has fewer guards, but more than I expected. I need someone who's already inside to shut down the energy shield for the delivery entrance. I'd hoped to figure out a way to get a prisoner to shut down the shield, but I'm afraid the place is locked up so tight that there's no way to contact any prisoners."

Gunn snorted. "You make shutting down a prison's energy shield sound like it's easy. Even if you could contact a prisoner, you'd probably be asking them to go on a suicide mission."

Bane shrugged and said, "Then I guess this is one job that I'll just have to walk away from. My ship's in a docking bay up the street. My client's pass codes should get me past the blockade again. Plenty of room on my ship. Anyone want to leave with me?"

"Wait!" Nuru said.

His mind raced. He desperately wanted to find his Master, but if the bounty hunter had described the situation accurately, it seemed they had little chance of breaking into the prison and successfully liberating any captives without getting someone hurt or killed. Unable to think of a solution, he lowered his head sadly.

And he found himself looking at the droid parts that remained strewn across the deck.

"Maybe none of us or any prisoners are the solution," he said. "Maybe what we need is a droid." He turned to Breaker. "You have a knack for technology." He gestured to the scrap on the floor. "Think you could assemble a single droid from these parts, and reprogram its brain to follow our orders?"

Breaker looked at the parts. "Shouldn't be difficult," he said, "but I'm guessing the brains are slave-circuited. They may not be reprogrammable. However . . . " He was still holding the head of Gunn's navigation droid, and he turned it over in his hands. "The Genetech brain could work." He looked at Gunn. "With your permission, of course."

"You got it," Gunn said. Then she looked straight at the navigation droid's head and said, "Sorry, Teejay, but you knew I was never the sentimental type."

Breaker said, "I'll need tools."

"I'll get them," Gunn said. "But let's get one thing straight. I'm not in this for fun. I expect someone here to help me get off this planet."

Nuru said, "We'll do everything we can. I promise."

As Gunn went to get a tool kit for Breaker, Bane smiled at Nuru and said, "You're very clever. Using a reprogrammed droid to break into the prison . . ." He shook his head. "I'm embarrassed that I didn't think of that idea myself."

In fact, ever since Bane had received his most recent instructions from Darth Sidious, he had gone to a great deal of trouble—summoning the four commando droids to fake the fight with him at Gunn's ship, and then pretending that he'd been temporarily blinded by a grenade—so Nuru would come up with that exact idea.

Bane had known it would be a risk to inform Nuru and the others that he was a bounty hunter. However, he also knew that it was easier to deceive someone by telling most of the truth than by telling a total lie.

CHAPTER 10

The new droid was constructed on a workbench that retracted from the cabin wall inside Lalo Gunn's transport. Even with Nuru's assistance, it took Breaker almost two hours to piece together a single droid commando from the gathered parts, and also to modify the inside of the assembly's metal cranium to make room for the Genetech navigation droid's brain.

When Breaker was finished putting all the pieces together, he made an adjustment to the back of the droid's head.

The droid's photoreceptors suddenly glowed white, and a small light on its chest went from black to red. Breaker stepped back from the workbench, turned to Nuru and said, "The Genetech brain's memory nodule was slightly damaged, but it appears to be compatible with the commando droid's programming, and it should obey our instructions."

"Will the droid still answer to the name Teejay?" asked Gunn.

"I don't know," Breaker said. "But he should operate on his own power. Let's test him out."

Just then, Knuckles, Chatterbox, Gunn, and the Duros bounty hunter walked up the landing ramp and entered the cabin. Both troopers were once again disguised in their robes. Nuru looked at them and said, "You saw the prison?"

Knuckles gestured to Bane and said, "It's just like he described it. The delivery entrance is shielded, but it has fewer guards. We checked out the bounty hunter's ship, too. It's in Docking Bay 21, and it's big enough to carry about twenty people. Is the droid ready?"

"We were just about to find out." Nuru returned his attention to the droid on the workbench and said, "Teejay? Can you hear me?"

There was a brief silence. The droid remained

completely motionless as he spoke through the grilled vocabulator at the base of his head. "You are . . . talking to me?"

"Yes," Nuru said. "Your name is Teejay."

"Is it?" The droid elevated his head, then pushed himself up to a seated position. "I did not know that."

Gunn said, "He doesn't even sound like Teejay anymore."

Nuru had noticed the change, too. Although he had not expected the refurbished droid to sound exactly like the waiter who had greeted him earlier, he was surprised that the droid's voice was so cold and mechanical, without any trace of emotion.

As the droid shifted his body, both Knuckles and Chatterbox raised their blaster rifles slightly, preparing to fire if necessary. Breaker saw his fellow troopers' action and said, "Stand down. He won't harm us."

Trusting Breaker, Knuckles and Chatterbox lowered their weapons.

"Teejay?" Gunn said. "Do you remember me?"

"Your voice is familiar," the droid said. He swung his legs off the workbench, placed his metal feet on the deck, and stood up. His head swung back and forth, looking at his arms as he flexed them. "Something is different," he said. "Was I always this way?"

"You were a navigation droid," Nuru said. "You're not anymore. Now, you're a fighter and a spy." He picked up a shock-stick that had been carried by one of the four droid commandos. "Do you understand?" He tossed the shock-stick to the droid.

The droid caught the blade weapon with one hand, looked at it, and then gave it a rapid spin with his nimble fingers. Then he released the weapon so that it spun in midair, caught it in his other hand, and swung it in a series of incredibly fast chops. The final chop brought the blade's energized tip within a millimeter of the deck before it stopped short. The droid cocked his head to the side. "I can fight," he said. "I can spy."

Gunn said, "He's definitely not Teejay anymore."

Knuckles said, "Then he needs a new name! The way he wields that blade, how about Cleaver?"

"Sounds good to me," Breaker said.

Gunn said, "You guys are really into nicknames, aren't you?"

"All right, then," Nuru said. "He's Cleaver." Facing the droid, he continued, "Cleaver, my name is Nuru. I'm a Jedi." Nuru signaled the three troopers to stand beside each other. "These soldiers are Knuckles, Chatterbox, and Breaker. You will obey our commands."

"Yes, Commander Nuru," the droid said with a polite bow as he held the shock-stick aside. "I will obey."

Bane gave Gunn the datatape that contained the prison's schematics. The group, including the newly named droid, reviewed the schematics on three small monitors at the transport's navigation console. The schematics showed the precise location of the factory level that had been converted into a cellblock for prisoners. Bane proposed a plan, which was as bold as it was devious.

When Bane was done talking, Nuru said, "You don't think we'll be able to disable the frequency jammer, too?"

Bane shook his head. "There isn't time. Our objective is to free the prisoners we're seeking and leave on my ship."

Gunn said, "I'm not crazy about leaving my ship behind."

Bane said, "I don't know any alternative. The pass codes are only good to get my ship through the blockade."

The three troopers looked at each other. Knuckles said, "What do you think about the plan, Breaker?"

"It'll be a walk in the park."

Chatterbox nodded in agreement.

"I have a question," Cleaver said, prompting everyone to look at him. "Am I to remain in the prison after you leave?"

"That's right," Bane said. "We need you to stay there to reactivate the energy shield after we're gone, to prevent other droids from following us."

"I understand," Cleaver said. There was a clicking sound at the back of his head, then he said, "While I am in the control room, what should I do if I am discovered?"

"Lock the door," Gunn said.

"And hope they don't have blasters," Bane added.

The droid's head clicked again, then he looked

at Nuru and said, "I understand."

Nuru tucked his lightsaber up his sleeve. Breaker pulled on his hooded robe while Knuckles and Chatterbox adjusted theirs to conceal their blaster rifles as well as their helmets. Cad Bane pulled on a poncho that hid his holstered pistols. Lalo Gunn tucked a compact blaster pistol into her right boot. As the group prepared to leave Gunn's ship, the droid's neck made another loud clicking noise.

"Just a moment," Breaker said. "I'd better oil Cleaver's neck and make sure it's properly aligned. Give me two minutes. I'll meet you outside."

Less than two minutes later, Cleaver's neck was no longer clicking. Breaker took a multitool from Gunn's kit, secured it to his belt, then pulled his hood up over his helmet and led the droid out of the transport to meet the others.

Nuru, Gunn, and Bane had no idea that Breaker, while oiling the droid's neck, had also let Cleaver in on a secret.

Except for the battle droid sentries that were

stationed outside, the KynachTech complex at the southern edge of the spaceport still looked more like a large factory than a prison. Wide sheets of metal were neatly stacked in a yard beside the building, which was topped by high windows and industrial ventilation chimneys, and the complex was bordered by warehouses. The tallest structure was the frequency-jammer tower, which jutted up from the side of the factory and resembled a pair of immense, shiny needles.

Nuru, Lalo Gunn, and Cad Bane led the three baggily disguised troopers past the warehouses near the factory's delivery entrance. All of them had their hands raised. Cleaver walked behind the group, holding a blaster rifle in one hand and a shock-stick in the other. The refurbished commando droid had the blaster rifle aimed at the troopers' backs.

As the group drew closer to the factory, one of the three troopers made a discreet hand signal to the other two, then quietly stepped away and ducked into an alley between two warehouses.

The trooper's departure went unnoticed by Nuru, Gunn, and Cad Bane, but not by Cleaver, who knew what the troopers were up to. Cleaver and the two remaining troopers kept their gazes forward and never broke their stride.

Four battle droid sentries stood in front of the delivery entrance, a wide open doorway that was sealed by an invisible energy shield. Nuru noticed two large, cylindrical gas tanks were mounted to the building's outer wall, to the right of the doorway.

As his group drew closer to the entrance, Nuru looked into the doorway to see a large chamber that contained a stack of storage containers and a stairway that traveled up alongside an elevated loading platform.

Four more battle droids were stationed on the platform, and two doors were visible at the top of the stairway. Remembering the bounty hunter's schematics, Nuru recalled that the door on the left was the control room.

Seeing all the battle droids, Nuru began to reconsider the bounty hunter's plan. He suddenly imagined any number of ways the plan might go wrong, but he knew that it was too late to turn back. He forced himself to remain calm as they came to a stop before the four droids outside the shielded entrance.

Cleaver said, "I am escorting these prisoners to processing."

The battle droid commander said, "But prisoners are to be escorted through the main entrance."

"These prisoners are low-security," Cleaver said. "My orders were to deliver them here because of a communications malfunction at the main entrance."

The droid commander said, "No one told us about a communications malfunction."

"The malfunction prevented anyone from telling you," Cleaver said.

"That makes sense," the droid said. He turned to face the droids on the landing platform and said, "Drop the shield!"

There was a buzzing sound as the energy shield deactivated. Cleaver said, "Move along."

Nuru led the procession through the doorway and into the chamber. Cleaver followed the group across the doorway's threshold, leaving the four battle droid sentries outside. There was another buzzing sound as the energy shield reactivated.

As the group moved into the chamber, there came a loud clatter from the loading platform.

Nuru, Gunn, Bane, and the two troopers looked up to see twelve additional battle droids appear on the platform. Nuru's hand darted for his lightsaber, but stopped short of grabbing it when he heard Gunn gasp as the doors at the top of the stairway opened to spill out more droids. All the droids trained their blaster rifles at the new arrivals.

"Looks like the clankers got us," one clone trooper said. "No point in disguises now." Both troopers tilted their heads back slightly, letting their hoods fall back to reveal their white plastoid helmets.

On the platform, the battle droids shifted and stepped aside, allowing an alien figure to emerge and gaze down on the people below. The alien was a tall Skakoan, and he wore metal-rimmed goggles and a face-concealing breath mask. Except for the top of his green-skinned head, his entire body was encased within a metal-armored pressure suit.

"Greetings, Republic dogs," the Skakoan said through his mask's voice synthesizer. "I am Overseer Umbrag of the Techno Union. I have been expecting you."

Expecting us? Nuru realized that someone in

his party might be a traitor. He looked at Gunn, who appeared to be as surprised as he was. Then he looked at the Duros bounty hunter, whose expression remained as impassive as ever. It wasn't until he glanced back behind him that he realized one of the three troopers was missing.

Before Nuru could even venture a guess as to which trooper had managed to avoid capture, Overseer Umbrag said, "Seize their weapons."

Nuru bent his knees and sprang high into the air, leaping so fast that the droids didn't even realize he'd jumped until he was already executing a midair somersault just below the ceiling. He was still tumbling as he drew his lightsaber from his belt. The battle droids' elbow joints clacked as they quickly raised their rifles, but not in time to fire at the boy, whose incredible leap carried him over and behind Overseer Umbrag. As Nuru's feet met the platform, he ignited his lightsaber so that its lethal blade was blazing within a hair of Umbrag's armored neck.

"Make one wrong move," Nuru said from behind Umbrag, "and you won't need your pressure suit any more."

CHAPTER 11

Umbrag heard the lightsaber's energized hum and saw its blade out of the corner of one goggled eye. Behind the goggles, both of his eyes had gone wide with surprise.

The battle droids who were closest to Umbrag and Nuru on the elevated loading platform tumbled away from their master to redirect their weapons at the blue-skinned boy. Nuru looked up at the back of Umbrag's head and held his lightsaber steady as he said, "Tell the droids to hold their fire."

"H-hold!" Umbrag gasped. "Hold your fire!"

Nuru said, "You were expecting us? Who told you?"

Before Umbrag could answer, a massive explosion sounded from outside the building. At the same time, the entire wall that surrounded the delivery entrance's energized doorway buckled and cracked, spraying dust across the chamber. The four droid sentries who had remained posted at the entrance were vaporized.

The power of the blast jolted everyone in the room, including Umbrag, whose sudden movement caused the side of his metal mask to come into contact with Nuru's lightsaber.

Umbrag flinched and shouted as he heard the hiss of melting metal. His gloved hands came up reflexively, and one hand struck the barrel of one battle droid's rifle. The startled droid fired the weapon into the ceiling.

The bounty hunter responded to the sound of blaster fire by quickly drawing both of his pistols and shooting at the metal heads of the nearest battle droids.

"No!" Nuru shouted. But it was too late. Shots had been fired, and Nuru heard the entire chamber erupt into chaos. He glanced past Umbrag's armored form to see the figures that stood on the floor below the loading platform.

Cleaver was using his rifle-wielding arm to mow down a trio of battle droids who'd been about to fire their own rifles into the backs of the two troopers, while, at the same time, he swung his shock-stick with the other hand to remove the heads of three more opponents. The two clone troopers had positioned themselves on either side of Gunn, shielding her as they faced away from each other and fired at the surrounding battle droids. Gunn had drawn her own blaster and was also shooting away.

Another explosion sounded from outside the building. Nuru's memory instantly flashed to the two cylindrical gas tanks that he'd noticed when his group had approached the entrance. He realized that someone—probably the absent clone trooper—had blown up both the tanks.

There was a bright flash as the entrance's energy shield crackled and died, causing Nuru to blink his red eyes. He was still positioned behind Umbrag on the loading platform when he adjusted his vision to look again to the floor below.

Cleaver was living up to his name by tearing into one battle droid after another. The troopers and

Gunn had maneuvered themselves behind the stack of storage containers, where Gunn had picked up a fallen droid's blaster rifle and was using that as well as her own pistol to return fire.

Where's the bounty hunter? Nuru couldn't see the Duros anywhere. But then he spotted three battle droids moving toward the edge of the platform, where they would all have clear shots at his allies below.

Nuru shoved past Umbrag and leaped at the three droids. His lightsaber swept through two while he was still airborne, neatly severing their heads before he landed and drove his blade straight through the third droid's torso. Then he heard a ratcheting sound from behind, and saw that the droids that remained on the platform were readying their blasters as they repositioned themselves around Umbrag.

The droids opened fire at Nuru. The young Jedi's blade became a rapid blur as he batted at the fired bolts and slammed them back at his attackers. Two droids fell, and then Nuru deftly sent two bolts straight to either side of the armored brace that encased Umbrag's neck, prompting the panicked Skakoan to yell, "Cease fire! Cease fire!"

But the droids didn't hear the command. They were still firing at the boy as he charged them, dodging the energy bolts as he brought his lightsaber through two droids, and then another two. Umbrag began backing away from the fight, moving toward a door at the back of the platform.

Nuru saw Umbrag's movement, but was still engaged with the droids and unable to stop him. As he felled the last droid on the platform, Umbrag was gone.

Just as suddenly as the fight had started, there was a loud energized snapping sound from the floor below the platform, and then the entire chamber went silent. Nuru ran to the platform's edge, looked down and saw Cleaver leading Gunn and the two troopers past a heap of shattered battle droids.

One trooper glanced up at Nuru and said, "You had us worried, Commander Nuru."

"I had *you* worried?" Nuru said as he deactivated his lightsaber. "Imagine my surprise when I realized we'd lost a trooper before we even got here!"

Gunn looked around and said, "Yeah, where's number three? If Chatterbox took off on me, I'll—"

"Chatterbox never left your side," the trooper

said as he gestured to the trooper next to Gunn.

Gunn turned to face Chatterbox's T-visored helmet and said, "Never left my side, huh? I *knew* you liked me."

"Breaker took a walk," Knuckles said.

"He is blowing things up," Cleaver said. "He told me he would."

Ignoring the droid, Nuru said, "Knuckles, what's going on? And where did the bounty hunter go?"

"We can talk about this later," Knuckles said. "More droids are probably on their way. If we're going to find our allies and get them out of here, we need to move now."

"You're right," Nuru said. "Let's just hope that the bounty hunter's schematics for this place were accurate, or we may never find the cell block level. Come on, Cleaver!" He turned and ran up the stairs that led out of the chamber. The others followed. They were still running up the stairs when they heard another explosion from somewhere outside.

What's Breaker doing?! Nuru thought.

Breaker hid behind a high stack of sheet metal as a squad of battle droids ran past him, heading for an outbuilding that had smoke pouring out of its upper windows.

After using his first explosive grenade to blow up the gas tanks outside the factory's delivery entrance, he had run fast to plant his second grenade on the side of the outbuilding's ventilation chimney. He didn't know how many droids were guarding the complex, but from what he could see, he had drawn their attention away from one particular place.

The frequency-jamming tower.

Breaker saw a drone gravsled—an automated flatbed cargo-carrier that floated on a cushion of air—transporting blocks of white plastoid across a landing pad. The gravsled was moving toward the tower that was his destination.

Keeping his helmeted head down and his eyes peeled for droids, Breaker quickly shrugged out of his robe and left it on the ground. Then he darted away from his hiding spot and jumped onto the side of the gravsled. His weight caused it to wobble slightly but it quickly righted itself and continued traveling forward through the air.

But a moment later, the gravsled slowed and came to a stop to allow five more battle droids to pass. Hearing the approaching droids, Breaker held his breath and remained perfectly still.

As the droids moved past the gravsled, one said, "Those explosions were loud, weren't they?"

A second droid said, "I heard they caused a communications malfunction."

A third droid said, "I heard the communications malfunction was a rumor started by the sentries at the delivery entrance."

A fourth droid said, "If we were having a communications malfunction, we would have heard about it."

A fifth droid said, "Unless a communications malfunction prevented us from hearing about it."

"I heard the explosions just fine," said the first droid.

"Who asked you?!" the four other droids said in unison.

None of the droids noticed the white armored figure that blended in perfectly with the shipment of plastoid blocks. After the droids walked off, the gravsled started up again. When it carried Breaker within two meters of the frequency-jammer tower, he dropped off the gravsled and made a crouching run for the tower's base.

There was a vent at the bottom of the tower. Breaker ducked and slid through the vent. It didn't take him long to find a control box. He reached for the multitool that he'd brought from Gunn's transport, removed his handheld comlink, and went to work as fast as he could. Using the multitool, he was easily able to disable the frequency jammer and use his own comlink to access the HoloNet and transmit a coded signal directly to the Jedi Temple on Coruscant.

Several minutes after fleeing the disastrous fight at the KynachTech Industries delivery chamber, Overseer Umbrag was breathless as he arrived in the shielded office suite that overlooked a landing platform, on which rested his private starship, a bulky Metalorn yacht.

Had he paused to look out his office's window, he would have seen dark smoke rising from one of the complex's outbuildings.

Umbrag's office contained a computer console that was linked directly to the frequency-jamming tower. His thick-gloved fingers trembled as he went to the console to adjust the controls that would enable a secure transmission over the HoloNet. He consulted a small monitor on the console, and was surprised to see that the monitor indicated that the HoloNet frequency was already open.

Umbrag turned to activate the holocomm on his desk. Blue light fizzled in the air above the holoprojector, and then the light flickered and formed into the three-dimensional image of a gaunt, dignified-looking man with a well-groomed white beard and intense eyes. The hologram said, "Yes?"

"Count Dooku!" Umbrag wheezed. "The Jedi . . . who came to Kynachi . . ."

"Yes, what of him? You haven't allowed him to escape, have you?"

"No!" Umbrag said. "You said he would be the only one. Another is here!"

Far across space, Dooku's brow furrowed, and his hologram in Umbrag's office did the same. Dooku said, "My informers told me only one Jedi would travel to Kynachi."

"I was expecting a few more clones," Umbrag said. "Not another Jedi! He is in my factory now!"

Dooku's head turned to his right, as if he were looking at someone or something else, and he nodded once before returning his gaze to Umbrag. Dooku said, "Are you aware that another transmission has left Kynachi?"

"What? That's impossible!"

Dooku scowled. "I have it on very good authority that a coded signal has just summoned Republic forces to Kynachi immediately. Evidently, your frequency jammer is no longer effective. I regret their assault ships will arrive before I can deliver reinforcements."

Umbrag gaped behind his metal mask, then stammered, "What—What shall we do?"

"Is the captured Jedi still alive?"

"Yes. He remains unconscious."

"Then leave him," Dooku said. "Destroy the factory, and withdraw your entire fleet from Kynachi at once."

"Destroy? Withdraw?" Umbrag sputtered behind his metal mask. "I have ten years invested in this factory!"

"The factory is expendable," Dooku said, "but we cannot afford to lose your fleet."

"Why don't I take the Jedi as a hostage?"

"Because the other Jedi will pursue you."

"But . . . ten years!"

"Overseer Umbrag, if you want to stay alive for another ten minutes, I advise you to follow my command. Leave. Now." Dooku broke the connection, and his hologram vanished.

Umbrag rushed to his Metalorn yacht. Although he was pained by the idea of blowing up the KynachTech factory, he knew better than to disobey Count Dooku, and he had every intention of triggering the auto-destruct system as soon as he was airborne.

Dooku stood in his secret lair in an industrial sector of Coruscant. Turning away from the holoprojector on the triangular table before him, he looked to the hunched, shadowy form of his Master, the Sith Lord Darth Sidious.

Dooku said, "Ring-Sol Ambase's apprentice appears to be living up to our expectations."

"Yes," Darth Sidious hissed. "Everything is proceeding as I have foreseen."

"Which trooper transmitted the signal from Kynachi?"

"CT-8863. His squad calls him Breaker." Then Darth Sidious leered, and he added, "They are *most* resourceful."

CHAPTER 12

The six battle droids who were stationed in the antechamber outside the lift tube in the factory's converted cell block level did not expect a droid commando to step out of the lift. But because the droid commando appeared to be a standard Federation model, the battle droids did not regard him or the weapons that he carried as a threat.

One of the battle droids noticed scorch marks on the droid commando's upper arms and torso, and said, "Looks like you've seen some action."

"Not enough," Cleaver said. He drove his shock-stick through the first droid as he raised his blaster-wielding arm and squeezed off five bursts at the others with pinpoint accuracy, blowing their heads clean off. The battle droids collapsed to the floor. Cleaver turned to face the lift tube's open door and said, "All clear."

Nuru, Gunn, Knuckles, and Chatterbox had pressed their bodies against the walls inside the lift to conceal themselves from the battle droids, and now they all slipped out through the lift's door to join Cleaver in the antechamber. The fallen droids lay on the floor near a wall-mounted computer console. Beyond the antechamber extended two long corridors with sealed metal doors.

Nuru looked at the computer console and said, "This probably controls the locks for the cell doors."

Knuckles said, "I'd bet that Breaker could probably hotwire it."

"But he's not here!"

Gunn snorted. "I'd bet that Breaker's not the only one handy with technology," she said as she stepped over a shattered droid to examine the console. A moment later, she was pressing buttons while watching numbers flash on an octagonal monitor.

Just then, Knuckles and Chatterbox heard a voice via their helmets' built-in comm units. "Breaker to Knuckles and Chatterbox. Do you copy?"

Knuckles raised a hand to the side of his helmet and said, "We copy." He turned to face Nuru and said, "It's Breaker."

Surprised, Nuru said, "I thought the comms were inoperative."

"Breaker disabled the frequency jammer," Knuckles said as he removed his handheld comm unit from his utility belt and gave it to Nuru.

"Breaker?" Nuru said into the comm. "Can you send a signal to Coruscant?"

"Already done, Commander," Breaker responded. "Is the bounty hunter still with you?"

"No. He pulled a vanishing act, but his schematics led us to the cell block. We're trying to release Master Ambase and the other—"

"Sir!" Breaker interrupted. "I'm in view of a landing pad outside the factory. A large ship is lifting off."

"What ship?"

"A Metalorn yacht."

Before Nuru could comment, a yellow light

winked on the computer console in front of Gunn. "That was easy," she said. "Fifty cells, all occupied."

Nuru said, "Open them all."

Gunn pressed a button and a loud pneumatic hiss sounded down from both corridors as the doors opened. A moment later, several golden-haired prisoners peered cautiously out from their cells. Nuru was about to call his Master's name when a violent explosion shook the entire cell block.

The enormous blast wracked the upper levels of the KynachTech factory, and, a moment later, the explosion's shock wave struck Breaker. He had left the disabled tower and had been moving stealthily along an access ramp near the landing pad, watching the Metalorn yacht ascend rapidly into the sky, when the shock wave launched him off his feet.

Breaker's lower body slammed against a metal guardrail at the edge of the ramp. He heard an ugly snap and felt a sudden, terrific pain shoot up through his left leg as his weight carried him over the guardrail and onto the ground below. He landed hard, his armor biting into him as he struck the ground and came to rest at the bottom of a ferrocrete wall.

Everything hurt. Breaker shifted his neck to look up and saw bright yellow flames and dark gray smoke rising from the factory. He tried to push himself up and immediately wished he hadn't.

"Breaker!" Knuckle's voice cried out over Breaker's helmet comlink. "What happened?"

"Big explosion," Breaker said through clenched teeth. "Don't know . . . what caused it. Factory's on fire." Breaker concentrated, pushing his pain out of his mind so he could focus on his memory of the bounty hunter's schematics. "Looks bad from out here. Don't leave by the lift tube. Take the emergency exit."

"We'll meet you outside."

Before Breaker could reply, there was another explosion directly overhead. Breaker's eyes were still open as the ferrocrete wall came crashing down on top of him.

Dust and small bits of mortar fell from the cell block ceiling as the next blast shook the building. Some of the prisoners ducked back into their cells while others leaped out into the corridors. Nuru had hoped to see his silver-haired Master, but there was no sign of Ring-Sol Ambase.

Knuckles positioned himself so he could see down both corridors, then said, "We're Republic Army troopers. If you're against the Federation, then you're with us!"

One of the prisoners said, "Republic Army?"

"That's right," Knuckles said. "Just call us the Breakout Squad."

A dark-haired man jumped out from one of the cells. Although he was clad in a simple, gray tunic and pants, his swarthy features betrayed his identity as a clone trooper. The clone called out, "Knuckles?"

"Trueblood!" Knuckles said. The last time he'd seen Trueblood was when he'd glimpsed him inside the escape pod with four other clones and General Ambase. "I'd know that face anywhere!"

Trueblood shouted, "Come on, men. It's not a trap. It's Knuckles!"

Three more gray-clad clones poked their heads

out of other cells. Knuckles recognized them as Close-Shave, No-Nines, and Sharp, who had been in the same escape pod as Trueblood. At the same time, more golden-haired prisoners, all natives of Kynachi, came pouring out of the other cells and shuffled past the clones, making their way toward the antechamber.

Knuckles looked at Trueblood and said, "Dyre didn't make it?"

"Killed by droids after our escape pod crash-landed and—look out!"

Knuckles turned fast, saw Cleaver moving in the antechamber, then turned back to the four startled clones and said, "Relax, fellas. That's Cleaver. He's on our side."

"A friendly droid commando?" Sharp said. "That's a new one to us!"

Nuru pushed his way past the Kynachi natives until he arrived at Knuckles's side. He looked up at Trueblood and the other gray-clad clones and said, "I'm Nuru Kungurama, Master Ambase's apprentice. Is he with you?"

Trueblood shook his head. "Sorry, we don't know where General Ambase is. There was a gas leak in our escape pod. Knocked us all out before we landed. The General was still unconscious when the droids overwhelmed us and killed Dyre. They took your Master away along with our armor after they brought us here."

Nuru grimaced, then bolted away from the clones. "Master Ambase! Master Ambase!" He darted into one empty cell, and then into the next, searching for any sign of the missing Jedi.

Another explosion sounded overhead, sending more dust and larger chunks of mortar down from the ceiling, and prompting several prisoners to cry out in alarm. Desperate to find his Master, Nuru ran back into the corridor and was about to enter the next empty cell when Knuckles grabbed him by the arm.

"Commander Nuru," Knuckles said, as dust rained down on his helmet. "We can't stay here. The ceiling's starting to buckle."

Despite the ceiling's impending collapse, Nuru calmed himself and reached out with the Force, hoping to sense his Master. Only then did he know the truth with certainty. Ring-Sol Ambase was gone.

Nuru pulled away from Knuckles and they

both quickly followed the rescued clones to the antechamber. As the four liberated clones arrived, they snatched up the blaster rifles from the floor beside the fallen battle droids.

"Move along, everyone!" Gunn shouted at the fleeing prisoners. "Don't worry about the droid commando, he's with us! Move, move, move!"

Despite Gunn's remark about Cleaver, the prisoners eyed the refurbished droid warily as they moved past it and followed Trueblood. Standing beside the droid, Chatterbox waved everyone toward the emergency exit, a doorway to a flight of stairs that led to an escape tunnel.

As Sharp hefted his newly acquired weapon, he saw the trooper who was directing the escapees to the exit. "Chatterbox!"

Chatterbox said, "Hi, Sharp."

Gunn's head turned as she heard Chatterbox's voice for the first time, and she said, "Quiet, you!" As she moved toward the exit, she saw Nuru and Knuckles were right behind her and said, "You're the last. Come on, move!"

Nuru and Knuckles ran for the exit. Knuckles saw Cleaver and said, "Don't just stand there! Run!"

A moment after Cleaver followed the others through the exit, the ceiling collapsed behind him. Dust blasted up the stairway, and Nuru found himself once again holding his breath with Knuckles by his side. They finally reached the escape tunnel, where the air cleared and Nuru was able to breathe again.

As they proceeded through the tunnel, Nuru said, "Knuckles, tell me what happened with the bounty hunter."

"I'm not sure," Knuckles said. "Breaker, Chatterbox, and I were suspicious of him from the start. But when he said there wasn't time to disable the frequency jammer, and also claimed that his pass codes were only good to get his ship through the blockade, we were certain he was up to something. Disabling the frequency jammer was the only way that we could summon help. And although it's generally illegal to transfer pass codes from one ship's transponder to another, it's not impossible."

"So, when did you work this out with the other troopers?"

"Remember what Breaker said when I asked him what he thought of the bounty hunter's plan?"

Nuru thought back. "Yes. He said it would be a

'walk in the park.' I thought that meant he thought the plan would be easy to pull off."

"It meant that Breaker saw an opportunity to break away from us so he could tackle the frequency jammer. And that's what he did. We couldn't tell you without alerting the bounty hunter. I don't know where he went, but one thing's for sure. He didn't bust anyone out of prison. We did that."

The tunnel's exit was an open bulkhead beside one of the factory's outbuildings, not far from the landing pad where Umbrag had fled in his Metalorn yacht. Trueblood, Close-Shave, and No-Nines led the golden-haired natives and assorted allies out of the tunnel.

Although the outbuilding was a good distance away from the larger factory building, the factory was such an inferno that the heat was almost unbearable.

Nuru, Knuckles, and Cleaver stepped outside. They had expected to encounter more battle droids, but the only ones they saw were lying on the ground, totally deactivated.

"What happened to the droids?" Nuru said.

"Breaker said he saw a ship taking off," Knuckles

said. "My guess is the whole Trade Federation blockade is gone, and they took their droid control ship with them. Without the control ship, these droids are just scrap metal."

Nuru glanced at Cleaver and said, "Then why are you still working?"

Cleaver pointed to his metal chest. "Breaker made me independent."

Nuru looked around. "Where is Breaker?"

"Hang on." Speaking into his helmet's comlink, Knuckles said, "Breaker? Breaker? Where are you?"

There was an awful moment of silence, then Breaker answered, "Knuckles . . . I'm done for. Get out of here."

Knuckles looked to Nuru and said, "Breaker's down."

"Do you know where?"

Knuckles consulted a sensor in his helmet, then pointed to a flaming pile of ferrocrete rubble below a wall near the vacant landing pad. "There."

Nuru looked at Cleaver, and saw that the droid was following Knuckles's gaze. Nuru said, "Find him."

Still carrying his shock-stick, Cleaver sprinted

off, running toward the rubble. Despite Knuckles's training, he yielded to some basic instinct and bolted after the droid commando.

"Stop, Knuckles!" Nuru shouted as Gunn and Chatterbox moved beside him. "It's too hot!"

Knuckles kept running. Cleaver arrived at the site first, but it was Knuckles who spotted Breaker's hand sticking out from under a ferrocrete block.

"Cleaver!" Knuckles said, ignoring the incredible heat. "Over here."

The droid drove his shock-stick into the ferrocrete and the block shattered. Knuckles plunged his hands into the rubble and began digging, tossing chunks of ferrocrete aside.

They quickly exposed one of Breaker's armored arms. Cleaver stabbed at the ferrocrete again, and Knuckles kept digging. In less than a minute, they hauled Breaker out of the rubble.

With Knuckles right behind him, Cleaver scooped Breaker up in his metal arms and ran back to the bulkhead. They found that the Kynachi natives had already gone, but Nuru, Gunn, Chatterbox, and the plainclothes clones were waiting for them.

Cleaver carefully placed Breaker on the ground.

Sharp said, "Breaker! I didn't expect to see you ever again either!"

As Nuru knelt and removed Breaker's helmet, Knuckles saw something move out of the edge of his own helmet's visor. He turned his gaze from his wounded ally and said, "Well, look who decided to rejoin us."

It was the Duros bounty hunter. He was walking away from one of the burning structures, moving straight toward Nuru and the others. Knuckles started to raise his blaster rifle at the approaching figure but Nuru reached out and grabbed the rifle's barrel, pushing it aside.

"Wait," Nuru said as he stood and moved away from Breaker's body.

"That bounty hunter's not to be trusted, Commander Nuru."

"I want to hear what he has to say."

Cad Bane came to a stop and said, "Sorry I ran out on you, but I wasn't getting paid to tangle with that many droids."

Nuru said, "Where'd you go? We know you never made it to the cell block."

"The prisoner I was hired to find was never in

the cell block," Bane said. "I'm afraid he was gone before I got here."

"So," Nuru said, "does that mean you're leaving empty-handed?"

"Looks that way." Bane turned his head and spat at the ground. Then he looked back at Nuru and said, "But that doesn't mean you have to leave the same way."

The bounty hunter moved one hand slowly toward the back of his belt. The clone troopers braced themselves, preparing to fire at him if he made one false move. But when the Duros's hand moved out from behind his back, he was holding something very unexpected. It was a lightsaber.

Bane did not activate the weapon, but took a cautious step closer to Nuru and held it out to him. "I found this while I was searching for my own quarry," Bane said. "I suspect it may have belonged to the Jedi you sought."

Nuru took the lightsaber. It was Ambase's weapon. He said, "Was there no other sign of him?"

"Only the lightsaber," Bane said. "For what it's worth, I hope you find him."

Nuru bowed his head slightly and said, "Thank you." As the bounty hunter started to turn and walk away, Nuru said, "What'd you say your name was?"

"I didn't," Bane said. He sauntered off, moving past the burning structures until he was gone.

Nuru secured his Master's lightsaber beside his own at his belt, then bent back down beside Breaker. "Breaker? Are you all right?"

"Leg's broken," Breaker said. "Three ribs, too. Other than that, I'm good to go."

Knuckles said, "Let's get him back to Gunn's ship."

Cad Bane guided the gravsled that he'd taken from the factory back to his starship at Docking Bay 21. On the gravsled rested a two-meter-long, black plastoid box with an array of sensors on its side. Bane lowered his ship's landing ramp and walked alongside the gravsled as he guided it into the main cabin.

Bane raised the landing platform, then went to

the ship's cockpit and initiated the launch sequence. A few minutes later, his ship was rising away from the Kynachi spaceport. When he reached space, he found that the Trade Federation blockade was gone.

Three Republic Navy *Venator*-class Star Destroyers suddenly dropped out of hyperspace to arrive in Kynachi's orbit. Bane's pass codes allowed him to avoid the Destroyers as easily as he had earlier bypassed the Federation blockade.

As the bounty hunter's ship sped away from Kynachi, Bane set the flight controls on autopilot and returned to the main cabin. Standing beside a console near the gravsled and the black plastoid box it carried, he activated a holocomm unit. Blue light flickered above the holoprojector, and formed into the image of the hooded Darth Sidious.

Darth Sidious said, "You have the body?"

"See for yourself," Bane said. He pressed a switch on the box's side, and the upper half of the box slid back silently to reveal a transparisteel coffin. Inside the coffin lay the body of Ring-Sol Ambase. His eyes were closed, and he wasn't moving.

Darth Sidious said, "The Jedi is alive?"

"That's what you paid me for." Bane pointed to

a life system monitor on the coffin's side and said, "He may not look it, but all his vital signs are good, even though he's not generating enough energy for another Jedi to detect him."

"Then his Padawan does not suspect you of anything?"

Bane grinned. "When I gave him his Master's lightsaber, he *thanked* me."

"Excellent."

"Where do you want the Jedi delivered?"

"To the fifth moon in the Bogden system," Darth Sidious said. "You will receive further instructions there." The Sith Lord broke the connection, and his hologram flickered out.

CHAPTER 13

"Master Ring-Sol Ambase's disappearance, most distressing this is," said the small, pointy-eared Jedi Master who appeared as a hologram above a console in Lalo Gunn's transport. "Also disturbing are your actions, young one."

Nuru stood before the console, facing the hologram of the Jedi Master Yoda. Behind Nuru, Breaker was sitting on the edge of Gunn's retractable workbench with tape wrapped around his ribcage and a bacta-filled medpac covering his left thigh.

Knuckles, Chatterbox, Gunn, and Cleaver were also in the cabin, silently watching Nuru's communication. Gunn's transport was still on

Kynachi, but now there were two Republic gunships resting on the ground beside it.

"I'm sorry, Master Yoda," Nuru said. "I know it's no excuse, but before my Master left Coruscant, I suddenly felt that he was in great danger. I believe it was the Force that guided my feelings. I only hoped that I might be able to help him."

"Informed the Jedi Council, you should have," Yoda said. "Not left the Temple as you did. A time of war, this is. You were . . . careless."

A second hologram appeared beside Yoda, and Nuru was surprised to see that it was Supreme Chancellor Palpatine.

"Please forgive me for interrupting, Master Yoda," Palpatine's hologram said. "But I have just received a report that Separatist forces attacked Ring-Sol Ambase's ship at Kynachi."

Yoda nodded. "Still missing, Master Ambase is."

"I offer you all my resources to help find him," Palpatine said. "I was also informed that members of Ambase's unit, the Breakout Squad, liberated Kynachi after a ten-year occupation by the Trade Federation."

Yoda nodded again. "Accomplish this, Breakout Squad did."

"An entire planet held captive for a decade," Palpatine said with a shudder. "Who is the commanding officer of the Breakout Squad?"

"Hrmm," Yoda said. He gave a sidelong glance at Palpatine, then gestured to the blue-skinned boy. "Chancellor Palpatine . . . to you I introduce Master Ambase's apprentice, Nuru Kungurama."

Nuru felt his throat go dry. He was not accustomed to the emotion of fear, but as Palpatine's hologram turned to face him, he was afraid that his time with the Jedi Order was about to come to an end.

Palpatine's eyebrows lifted. "You are a Chiss!"

Nuru was taken aback, but he replied, "Yes, Chancellor."

"What an amazing coincidence. An hour ago, an ambassador of the Chiss Ascendancy contacted my office, requesting to meet with a representative of the Jedi Order at a Chiss space station as soon as possible."

Palpatine looked at Yoda and said, "The Republic cannot ignore this opportunity for diplomatic relations with the Chiss. Because the Separatists may have spies in Chiss space, I propose a classified mission. Master Yoda, with your permission, might Nuru Kungurama be available to meet with this ambassador?"

Nuru had thought that the Chancellor was going to reprimand him, not propose sending him on a mission. He could hardly believe his ears. He had been an infant when he first arrived at the Jedi Temple, and had no memory of his homeworld. In fact, few people in the Republic knew anything about the Chiss.

The Chiss lived in the Unknown Regions, far beyond the Outer Rim, and had no official affiliation with the Republic. Even the vast Jedi Archives had little data about the blue-skinned, red-eyed humanoids. Although Nuru had been raised to serve the Jedi Order, he could not help being curious about his place of origin.

Nuru swallowed hard. He had never imagined that he might one day travel to Chiss space.

"Hrmm," Yoda said again. "About the Chiss, little do we know. For a secret mission, a more experienced Jedi, the Council should send."

"But who else is available?" Palpatine said. "It would be most unfortunate if we failed to take advantage of this opportunity. I've no doubt that the Chiss ambassador would be very pleased to meet with a Chiss Jedi, even one so young. Perhaps an escort could be arranged?"

"Accompany Nuru, Breakout Squad could," Yoda mused aloud. "But to other worlds, our ships must go."

Behind Nuru, Gunn cleared her throat. Nuru glanced at her and she aimed a thumb at herself. She said, "You get the coordinates, I'll get you there."

Returning his gaze to Yoda's hologram, Nuru said, "A freelance pilot has volunteered to deliver me and Breakout Squad to Csilla."

"Well done, Nuru Kungurama," Palpatine said. "I have every faith that your mission will be a success. The coordinates for Csilla will be transmitted to your ship immediately."

Yoda nodded to Nuru and said solemnly, "May the Force be with you."

Nuru bowed, and then the two holograms vanished.

"All right, then," Gunn said. "Gunn's Diner is

officially closed. It's time for the *Hasty Harpy* to leave this dull rock."

She glanced at Cleaver, then looked at Knuckles and said, "Does the droid have to come with us?"

"Cleaver helped save Breaker! Far as I'm concerned, he's part of Breakout Squad, too."

As Breaker carefully pulled on his black body glove, he said, "I'll second that. Cleaver's a keeper."

Cleaver said, "Thank you, Master Breaker."

Gunn shook her head. "You're all crazy." She was about to raise the landing platform when a fully armored clone trooper came running up the ramp and into the cabin.

"Permission to board?" said the trooper.

"Granted," Gunn said. "Whoever you are."

Chatterbox said, "He's Sharp. Can't you tell?"

Gunn glared at Chatterbox and said, "You're starting to talk too much."

Sharp turned his helmeted head to face the young Jedi and said, "I just received orders to join your unit, Commander Nuru."

"Good to have you with us, Sharp."

"I've got the coordinates for our destination," Gunn said as she raised the landing ramp. "Everyone find a seat and buckle in."

Nuru belted himself into a seat beside Breaker. "Feeling any better?" the young Jedi asked.

"Much," Breaker replied. "I'm just sorry we lost General Ambase."

Nuru bit his lower lip, then said, "He's still alive, Breaker. I know he is. I just wish I knew where to find him."

Breaker gestured to the other troopers and said, "The boys and I will do everything we can to help you."

"Thanks, Breaker," Nuru said. "I'm fortunate to have all of you watching my back."

"That's what we're here for, Commander." Then Breaker lowered his voice and added, "But let's not forget that we still don't know how the Separatists knew we'd be arriving at Kynachi, or who sabotaged our escape pods. We may still be in danger, and I urge you to be watchful, too."

"You can count on it," Nuru said.

The *Hasty Harpy*'s thrusters ignited and the ship lifted off. Minutes later, the ship leaped into hyperspace, heading for the Unknown Regions.

For the 501st New England Garrison—R.W.

NEXT:

Star Wars: The Clone Wars
Secret Missions #2:
Curse of the Black Hole Pirates

On their first official assignment to a distant world in the Unknown Regions, the young Jedi Nuru Kungurama and the newly-formed Breakout Squad take an unexpected and very dangerous detour. Suddenly overwhelmed by space pirates, the members of Breakout Squad become convinced that a traitor is in their midst. Meanwhile, far across the galaxy, the Sith Lords attempt to enlist a Jedi to help them with their dark schemes.

ABOUT THE AUTHOR

A former editor of *Star Wars* and *Indiana Jones* comics, Ryder Windham has written more than sixty books, including *Star Wars: The Ultimate Visual Guide* (DK Publishing), *Star Wars: The Life and Legend of Obi-Wan Kenobi* (Scholastic), and *Indiana Jones and the Pyramid of the Sorcerer* (Harper Collins UK and Scholastic). He lives in Providence, Rhode Island, with his family.

ABOUT THE COVER ARTIST

Wayne Lo served as Art Director on the video game *Lair* as well as spent six years in Industrial Light & Magic's art department, where he cursed pirates, skinned werewolves, skewered vampires, and thawed Neverland, before joining the design team for Lucasfilm's *Star Wars: The Clone Wars* animated series.